BOUND TO HER GREEK BILLIONAIRE

BY

REBECCA WINTERS

First Published in Great Britain 2017
By Mills & Boon, an imprint of HarperCollins*Publishers*
1 London Bridge Street, London, SE1 9GF

ISBN: 978-0-263-06932-7

Our policy is to use papers that are natural, renewable and recyclable products and made from wood grown in sustainable forests. The logging and manufacturing processes conform to the legal environmental regulations of the country of origin.

Printed and bound in Great Britain
by CPI Antony Rowe, Chippenham, Wiltshire

Rebecca Winters lives in Salt Lake City, Utah. With canyons and high alpine meadows full of wildflowers, she never runs out of places to explore. They, plus her favourite vacation spots in Europe, often end up as backgrounds for her romance novels—because writing is her passion, along with her family and church. Rebecca loves to hear from readers. If you wish to email her, please visit her website at cleanromances.com.

Books by Rebecca Winters

Mills & Boon Romance

The Billionaire's Club

Return of Her Italian Duke

The Vineyards of Calanetti

His Princess of Convenience

The Montanari Marriages

The Billionaire's Baby Swap
The Billionaire Who Saw Her Beauty

Greek Billionaires

The Millionaire's True Worth
A Wedding for the Greek Tycoon

The Billionaire's Prize

Visit the Author Profile page
at millsandboon.co.uk for more titles.

To my first editor and friend, Paula Eykelhof,
who believed in my writing and helped me find
a happy home at Mills & Boon Romance.
I've been there ever since.
How blessed could an author be?

CHAPTER ONE

LYS THERON ARRIVED ahead of time for her appointment with the detective at the prefecture in Heraklion, Crete. The officer at the desk looked her over in a way she found insulting and hurtful.

From her early teens she'd had to get used to men young and old staring at her. But his scrutiny was different because the unexpected and unexplained death a month ago of Nassos Rodino, the Greek multimillionaire hotelier on Crete, continued to be under police investigation and she was one of several people still being questioned.

The well-known, forty-nine-year-old owner of the Rodino Luxury Hotel and Resort in Heraklion had died too young. Nassos had always been an object of fascination in the news. But since the divorce from his wife, Danae, four months ago, there'd been rumors that he'd been having an affair with twenty-six-year-old Lys, his former ward who'd lived in their household since the age of seventeen.

While Lys struggled with her grief over his death, and many people lamented his demise, the media had done their best to sensationalize it, developing a story that had played every night in the television news cycle. Had Lys conducted a secret affair with the famous hotelier for several years? Questions had been raised as to what had actually caused the divorce and his ultimate death.

Without answers, speculation grew that foul play might have been involved. Rumor that Lys might have caused his death to gain access to part of his money had caught hold. Though the detective conducting the investigation hadn't put the blame on anyone, the reason for Nassos's death still hadn't been declared and a cloud hung over her. Lys's heart shuddered over the cruel gossip. Nassos was the man she'd loved like a father since childhood.

At seventeen, her millionaire Greek father, Kristos Theron, owner of a successful hotel in New York City, had been killed in a small plane accident. He'd left a will with a legal stipulation. If he died before she was of age, his best friend and former business partner, Nassos Rodino, would become her legal guardian.

Nassos had come to New York often throughout her early childhood and she had seen him as part of her extended family. When her father died, it was no hardship to travel to Greece with him.

But the moment Nassos had brought her to his home, she'd discovered that he and his wife had been living in a troublesome marriage.

Lys had never known the reason for their struggles, but it grieved her because she'd sensed that deep down they loved each other. It was all very complicated and she'd tried not to add to their problems. But in that regard she felt she'd failed when she'd started dating men neither of them approved of.

Nassos called them rich men's playboy sons.

Danae saw them as opportunists with no substance, adding to Lys's insecurity that somehow she didn't have the ability to attract the right kind of man. None of her relationships developed into anything serious because she sensed her adoptive parents' disapproval.

Since coming to live with them, the paparazzi had followed her around, never missing a chance to exploit her private life by filming her accompanied by any rich man she may have been seen with in public. Unfortunately in her work at Nassos's exclusive hotel chain, wealthy people made up her world. She'd never known anything else.

If she'd met and fallen in love with a poor fisherman, would they have approved of her choice? She didn't have an answer to that question, nor to the many others that she often thought of as Lys suffered from a lack of confidence. Having lost her mother at the age of nine hadn't helped.

Their disapproval hurt her terribly because she'd loved Nassos and his wife so much and wanted their acceptance. Lys's father had entrusted her to Nassos. Right now she felt like she'd let down three of the most important people in her life, but not on purpose.

Though he and Danae had suffered marital difficulties, they'd been wonderful to Lys and had made life beautiful at their villa on Kasos Island while she'd dealt with her sorrow. They'd helped her through those difficult years and had made it possible for her to go to college on the mainland.

Nassos was the kindest, dearest man Lys had ever known in her life next to her own father. The two men had been born on Kasos and had always been best friends. Early in their lives they'd gone into the fishing business together and had slowly amassed their fortunes. Kristos had ended up in New York, while Nassos stayed on Heraklion and had eventually married.

For Lys, the underlying strife during their divorce had been devastating. Since then she and Danae had been estranged. It tore her heart out. At this point Lys didn't know how to overcome her pain except to pour herself into work at the hotel, and avoid the press as much as possible.

Deep in tortured thoughts, she heard a voice. "Kyria Theron?" She lifted her head to see another officer in the doorway. "Thank you for coming. Detective Vlassis will see you now."

Hopefully this meeting would provide the answer that let her out of proverbial jail and allowed the funeral to take place. She walked inside.

"Sit down, Kyria Theron."

Lys found a chair opposite his desk.

"Coffee? Tea?"

"Neither, thank you."

The somber detective sat back in his chair tapping the tips of his long fingers together. "I have good news for you. The medical examiner has turned over his findings to my office. We know the truth and foul play has been ruled out."

"You're serious?" Her voice shook. The rumor that she might have poisoned Nassos with some invisible drug in his penthouse apartment in order for her to get a portion of his money had been devastating for her.

"It's been determined he died of a subarachnoid hemorrhage probably caused from an earlier head injury."

"Why did it take so long?" she cried.

"Unfortunately the bleeding went undetected. The reason it was difficult to find the first time was because it's not unusual for SAH to be initially misdiagnosed as a migraine."

"So the doctor didn't catch it."

"Not at first. A human mistake. It caused a delay in obtaining a CT scan."

A small gasp escaped her lips. "After he'd hit his head on the kitchen cupboard several months ago, I thought he must have suffered a concussion. I told him I wanted to talk to his doctor about it, but Nassos told me to stop fussing because the pain went away. That must be why he had a stroke." Tears rolled down her cheeks. "Thank heaven he can now be laid to rest."

"This has been a very stressful time for you, but it's over. The press has been informed. I'm sorry for your loss and wish you well in the future."

Another miracle. "Thank you. Have you told his ex-wife?"

"Yes."

"Good." Now Danae could make the funeral arrangements. "You'll never know what this means to me."

Lys jumped up from the chair. "Thank you." She couldn't leave the police station fast enough and rushed past the officer posted at the front desk without glancing at him. She couldn't endure one more smirk.

Once outside, Lys hurried to her car, running past the usual news people stalking her movements to take pictures. She got into her car and drove back to the

Rodino Luxury Hotel where she had her own suite. She'd been living there and working in the accounts department for Nassos since graduating from business college in Heraklion four years ago.

The moment she reached her room on the third floor, she flung herself across the bed and sobbed. It was over at last. But with Nassos's death and Lys's unwanted estrangement with his ex-wife, there was no one to pick up the emotional pieces.

The couple's tragic divorce had fragmented Lys. If they'd been going to end their marriage, why hadn't it happened years before now? She simply didn't understand. And then had come the shocking news of his death... The loss was almost more than she could bear.

They'd worked together at the hotel. He'd taught her everything about the business. He'd been her friend, confidant, mentor. How was she going to be able to go on without him?

For Nassos not to be there anymore was killing her and she missed Danae terribly. Until the police had closed the case, Lys had been in limbo, trying to do her usual job, but her mind and heart hadn't been there. When she did have to leave the hotel for any reason, she'd felt accusatory stares coming in all directions and avoided any publicity if she could help it.

Thankfully this was over and there'd be an end to the malicious talk that he'd been murdered. Hopefully everything would die down, but where did she go from here? Lys felt like she'd been driving her car when the steering wheel had suddenly disappeared, leaving her to plunge over a cliff. She was so heartbroken she could hardly think.

While in this state, the phone rang. Lys turned over to look at the caller ID. It was Xander Pappas, Nassos's attorney. She picked up and learned that he'd be in Nassos's private office at the hotel in a half hour to talk to her. The detective had already been in touch with him.

"I have something important to give you."

She sat up in surprise. "Will Danae be meeting with us?" Lys longed to talk to her.

"No. We've already spoken and I've read her the will. She'll be calling you about the funeral."

"I see."

Stabbed with fresh pain, Lys thanked him and hung up. If there hadn't been a divorce, she and Danae would have planned his funeral together. Now everything had changed. More tears gushed down her cheeks before she got off the bed to freshen up.

Of course she hadn't expected to be present at the reading of the will and hadn't wanted to be. Danae had been married to Nassos for twenty-four years. That business was between the two of them.

A few minutes later she left for the corporate office downstairs. On the way, she couldn't help but wonder what Xander wanted to give her. Nassos couldn't have known when he would die, so she couldn't imagine what it was.

After nodding to Giorgos, the annoying general manager of the hotel, she walked in to Nassos's private office. The attorney greeted her and told her to sit down.

"I have two items to give you. Both envelopes are sealed. You'll know what to do after you open the envelope marked Letter first. Nassos wrote to you at the time he divorced Danae." He put both envelopes on the desk.

She swallowed hard. Nassos had written something that recently? "Have you read it?"

"No. He gave me instructions to give them both to you upon his death, whenever that would be. Who would have imagined he'd die this early in his life? I'll miss him too and am so sorry since I know how close you two were. I'll leave now. If you have any questions, call me at my office."

After he left the room, Lys reached for the envelope and pulled out the letter with a trembling hand. She knew Nassos's handwriting. He wrote with a certain panache that was unmistakable.

My dearest little Lysette,

Immediately her eyes filled with more tears.

I'll always think of you that way, no matter how old you are when you read this letter. You're the daughter I never had. Danae and I couldn't have children. The problem was mine. I found out early in our marriage that I was infertile. It came as a great shock, but I'd dreamed of having children, so I wanted to adopt. She didn't, and I could never talk her into it. I decided she didn't love me enough or she would have agreed to try because I wanted children more than anything.

Six months ago, Xander let me know that he knew of a baby we could adopt. I went to Danae and begged her. It could be our last chance, but she still said no. In my anger I divorced the woman I loved and always will. Now I'm paying for it dearly because I don't believe she'll forgive me.

You need to know that you were never the reason for our marital troubles. I ruined things at the beginning of our marriage by making an issue that she stay at home. I insisted she quit her job because I was raised with old-fashioned ideas. I was wrong to impose them on Danae. She's very much a modern woman and a part of me resented the fact that she couldn't be happy at home.

Please realize that your coming to us helped keep our marriage together and deep down she knows it. I'm afraid it was because of my damnable pride—my greatest flaw—nothing more, that made me divorce her, so never ever blame yourself. If I was hard on you because of the men you dated, it was only because of my desperate fear you might end up in a bad marriage with a man who didn't value you enough. Danae felt the same way.

Forgive us if we hurt you in any way.

"Oh, Nassos—" Lys cried out in relief and anguish.

You have a massive inheritance from your father that will be given to you on your twenty-seventh birthday. He dictated that specific time in his will to make sure you'd be mature enough when you came into your money.

Lys was incredulous. She'd thought it had all been incorporated into the Rodino empire. Nassos would have deserved every euro of it.

> Again, I have no idea how old you are now that I'm dead. I suspect you're a very wealthy woman, hopefully married with children, maybe even grandchildren. And happy!
>
> As you will have found out from Danae, she inherited everything with one exception...the hotel is your inheritance from me to own and run as you will.

Lys reeled physically and clung to the arms of the chair.

No. It wasn't possible. The hotel should have been given to Danae, who understood the hotel business very well. It was Nassos who'd hired her away from another hotelier to come and work for him twenty-four years ago. How sad that even after his death, Nassos couldn't allow her to continue in a career she'd enjoyed.

Lys's eyes closed tightly for a moment.

Danae hadn't contacted Lys yet. There hadn't been time. How could Nassos have done this to the woman he'd loved? Wiping her eyes, she went on reading.

> But you're not the sole owner, Lys.

What? The shocks just kept coming.

> Before you take possession, you must give the sealed envelope to Takis Manolis. You've

heard me and Danae talk about him often enough. When he came to Crete periodically, we'd discuss business on my yacht where we could be private. I never did believe in mixing my business matters with my personal life. The two don't go together.

You'll know where to find him when the time comes. The two of you will share ownership for six months. After that time period, you'll both be free to make any decisions you want.

By the time you read this, he's probably married with children and grandchildren too. I've thought of him as the son I never had.

It was my thrill and privilege to be your guardian, friend and adoptive father for the child of my best friend Kristos.

Love always,

Nassos.

You can't go home again.

Whoever coined the phrase was wrong. Yes, you could go home again.

In the last eleven years, Takis Manolis had made four trips a year to Crete and nothing had changed… Not the pain, not the landscape, not his family.

Naturally they were all a little older each time he flew here from New York and later from Italy, but everything had stayed the same if you looked at the inner vessel.

The village of Tylissos where he'd been born was still situated on the northeastern mountainside of Psiloritis near the sea. Time hadn't altered it a whit.

Nor had it altered the views of Takis's father or his elder brother, Lukios, who helped their father run the old ten-room hotel.

His family followed the philotimo creed for all Cretans to maintain their unflappable dignity even if their existence bordered on poverty when the hotel didn't fill. They respected the rich and didn't try to become something greater than they were. Takis was baffled that they didn't mind being poor and accepted it as their lot in life.

Until recent years there'd been very little inherited wealth in Greece. Most of the Greek millionaires were self-made, but envy wasn't part of his brother's or his father's makeup.

Takis's older sister, Kori, married to a cook at one of the village restaurants where she worked, didn't have to tell him that she and her husband, Deimos, struggled to make a decent living.

They had a little girl, Cassia, now three years old, who'd been in and out of the hospital after her birth because of chronic asthma and needed a lot of medical care. He was thankful that at least Kori kept the cash he'd given her for a belated birthday present, knowing she'd use it for bills.

Though the family accepted the gifts he brought whenever he came, pride prevented his father from taking any monetary help. Lukios was the same. Being a married man with a wife and two children, who were now four and five, he would never look to Takis for assistance to make life a little easier for his family and in-laws.

This centuries-old pride thwarted Takis's heartfelt need and desire to shower his family with all the things of which they'd been deprived and caused him deep grief.

Early in life he'd known he was different from the rest of them, never going along with their family's status quo. Though he'd never openly fought with his father or brother, he'd struggled to conform.

His mother knew how he felt, but all she could do was urge Takis to keep the peace. When he'd told her of his dreams to go to college to better himself, she'd said it was impossible. They didn't have the money. None of the Manolis family had ever gone for a higher education.

Takis just couldn't understand why neither his father nor brother didn't want to expand and grow the small hotel that had been handed down from an earlier generation. He could see nothing wrong with trying to build it into something bigger and better. To be ambitious didn't make you dishonorable, but his father and brother weren't risk takers and refused to change their ways.

There were times when he wondered if he really was his parents' birth child. Except that his physical features and build proclaimed him a Manolis through and through.

By his midteens, Takis had feared that if he stayed on Crete, he would turn into his brother, who was a clone of the Manolis men before him, each having so little to show for all their hard work. More and more his ideas clashed with his father's over how to bring in more clients and build another couple of floors on the hotel.

Takis had worked out all his ideas in detail. One day he'd approached his father in all seriousness, wanting to talk to him man-to-man. But when he made his proposals, his father said something that stopped him cold.

Your ideas do you credit, my son, but they don't reflect my vision for our family business. One day you'll be a man and you'll understand.

Understand what?

Pierced by his father's comment, Takis took it to mean his ideas weren't good enough and never would be, even when he became a man.

At that moment something snapped inside Takis. He determined to go to college despite what his mother had said.

So he bought a secondhand bike and after helping his father during the week on a regular basis, he rode the few kilometers to his second job at the famous Rodino hotel and resort in Heraklion on weekends to earn extra money. The manager was soon impressed with Takis's drive. In time he introduced him to the owner of the hotel, Nassos Rodino, who had several talks with Takis about his financial situation.

One day the unimaginable had happened. Kyrie Rodino called him to his office and helped him apply for a work visa and permit to travel to New York. His best friend, Kristos Theron, the owner of a successful hotel in New York City, would let Takis work for him. He could make a lot more money there and go to the kind of college that would help him get ahead in the business world. He'd improve his English too.

Takis couldn't believe anyone would do something so fantastic for him and returned home to tell his parents about the opportunity.

His mother kept quiet. As for his father, he listened

and nodded. *If this is what you want to do, then you must do it.*

But how do you feel about it, Baba*?* Takis had still wanted his father's approval.

His father shrugged his shoulders. *Does it matter? You're eighteen years old now and are in charge of your own destiny. At eighteen a man can leave his father and make his own way.*

That isn't the answer I was hoping for. His father hadn't given him his blessing and probably resented Nassos Rodino for making any of this possible.

If you're a man, then you don't need an answer.

Takis had felt rebuked. His mother remained silent as he left the room with a hurt too deep to express. After the talk with his father, he'd had the feeling his parent had already felt abandoned before he'd even approached him.

Combined with the pain of having recently lost his girlfriend, who'd been killed in a bus accident, he finally made the decision to leave home. She'd been the one he could confide in about his dreams.

After all their talks, she'd known he'd been afraid to leave his family in case they thought he was letting them down. But she'd encouraged him and told him to spread his wings. They'd talked about her joining him in New York at a later date.

With her gone, he'd had no one who understood everything going on inside him. Her compassion had made her such an exceptional person, and he'd never found that incredible quality in the women he'd met since leaving Crete.

In the end, he'd made the decision to go after the opportunity that would enrich his life and he vowed, one day, that he would return and help his family in every capacity possible.

That was a long time ago.

On this cool March day, he held in the tears as he embraced his mother one more time. On this trip he noticed she'd aged and hadn't exhibited her usual energy. That troubled him. "I promise I'll be back soon."

"Why don't you come home to live? You can afford it. We miss you so much." Her tears tugged at his heart.

His father didn't weep, but Takis detected a new sorrow in his eyes. Why was it there? Why didn't his parent speak the words of love and acceptance he longed to hear?

"Do what you have to do." Those were similar to the words he'd said to Takis before he'd left for New York eleven years ago. "Be safe, my son."

But his father still hadn't been the one to ask him to come home or tell him he'd like him to work at the hotel with the family again. Had Takis done irreparable damage to their relationship?

"You too, *Baba*." His throat had swollen with emotion. "Stay well."

He turned to his mother once more. Was the sorrow he'd seen in his father's eyes over concern for his wife? Was there something wrong with her? With his father? Something no one in the family was telling him?

This visit had troubled him with thoughts he didn't want to entertain. He hugged everyone and kissed his nieces and nephews. Then he climbed into the taxi in front of the family-owned hotel that needed refurbishing. Heaven knew it needed everything. *They* needed everything.

His eyes clung to his mother's once more. *Had she been trying to tell him something?* He blew her a kiss.

The flight to Athens would be leaving from Heraklion airport in four hours. First he would attend the funeral services for Nassos Rodino at the Greek Orthodox church in the heart of Heraklion. The recently divorced hotel owner, rumored to have a mistress, had suffered a stroke in the prime of his life—a stroke that had preceded his death. This had shocked Takis, who'd met with the man, who had given him so much, on his yacht to talk business when Takis had last come to Crete.

Most important to Takis was that he owed the hotelier a debt that bordered on love. His gratitude to the older man knew no bounds.

In truth he couldn't think of another successful man who would have gone to such lengths to give Takis the chance to better himself, even to go as far as sponsoring him in the United States.

Once the funeral was over, he'd fly to Athens. From there he'd take another flight to Milan, Italy, where he was part owner, and manager of the five-star Castello Supremo Hotel and Ristorante di Lombardi.

But all the way to the church his mother's words rang in his ears. *Why don't you come home to live. You can afford it.* His mother had never been so outspoken in her thoughts before.

Yes, he could afford it. In the eleven years he'd been away, he'd made millions while his family continued to eke out their existence.

Was she telling him something without coming

right out and saying it? Was she ill? Or his father? Death with dignity? Never saying a word? *Damn that pride of theirs if it was true!*

Neither Kori nor Lukios had said anything, but maybe his siblings had been kept in the dark. Then again maybe nothing was wrong and his mother, who was getting older, was simply letting him know how much they'd missed him.

He missed them too. Of course he'd come back in an instant if they needed him. But to come home for good? Even if his two business partners were in agreement and bought him out—even if he sold his hotel chain in New York, would his father allow him to work alongside him? What if he refused Takis's help? What would Takis do for the rest of his life? Build a new hotel conglomerate on Crete?

His eyes closed tightly. He could never do that to his father and use the Manolis name. A son honored his father and showed him respect by never taking anything away from him.

Two years ago Takis had built a children's hospital in his hometown village of Tylissos on Crete in order that his niece Cassia would get the kind of skilled medical help she needed. The hospital gave free medical care with no child turned away.

He'd kept his dealings anonymous, using local people who had no idea Takis had funded everything including the doctors' salaries. It helped him to know he was doing something for his family, even if they weren't aware of it.

Long ago Takis had lost hope that one day his father might be proud of him for trying to make something of his life in order to help them. His parent had never been anything but kind to him, but deep in his heart lived the fear that his family had always compared him to their ever faithful Lukios and would never see Takis in the same light.

In his pain he needed to get back to Italy and ask advice from his partners, who were as close to him as brothers.

"Kyrie?" The taxi driver broke in on his tormented thoughts by telling him they'd arrived at the corner of the square.

Takis had been in a daze. "If you'll wait here, I'll be back in an hour." He handed him some bills and got out to join a crowd of people entering the church, where the covered coffin faced east.

Once he found a seat, he listened to the white-robed priest who conducted the service. After leading them in hymns and scriptures, the priest asked God to give Nassos rest and forgive all his sins. As far as Takis was concerned, the man had no sins. Because of him, Takis had been given a precious gift that had changed his life completely. But at what price?

Soon the bereaved, dressed in black, started down the aisle to go to the cemetery. One dark-haired woman in a black veil appeared particularly overcome with sorrow. Nassos's ex-wife? Takis had never met her. Nassos had kept their few meetings totally private.

Because he'd arrived late, he'd taken a seat on the aisle at the back. While he waited for everyone to pass, his gaze happened to fasten on probably the most gorgeous young dark-blonde woman he'd ever seen in his life.

Her two-piece black suit provided the perfect foil

for her stunning classic features only rivaled by violet eyes. Their color reminded him of the Chaste plant belonging to the verbena family that grew all over Crete. They peered out of dark lashes that took his breath. But he could see she was grief stricken. Who *was* she?

He turned his head to watch her walk out the rear of the church. If he weren't going to be late to catch his flight, he'd drive to the cemetery and find out her name. Hers was a face and figure he would never forget, not in a lifetime.

CHAPTER TWO

FIVE DAYS AFTER the funeral, Lys left Giorgos, the manager of the Rodino Hotel, in charge. The paparazzi took pictures as she climbed in the limo taking her to the airport for her flight to Athens. It connected to another flight to Milan, Italy. Her destination was the Castello Supremo Hotel and Ristorante di Lombardi.

In the year before her father's death, she'd heard her father and Nassos talking about a new employee at her father's hotel named Takis Manolis. Nassos had made it possible for the younger man from Crete to get a work visa and go to college in the United States while working at her father's hotel in New York. Lys's understanding was that he was exceptional and showed real promise in the hotel industry.

Their interest had piqued *her* interest, but she'd never met him since she and her father had lived in their own home in the city. She'd rarely gone to the hotel for any reason.

After her father's death, and the move to Crete to Nassos and Danae's villa on Kasos, the name of Takis came up again. Nassos spoke fondly of him and she learned more about him. The Manolis teen had come from Tylissos and had needed help to escape a life that was close to the poverty line.

When Lys asked Nassos why he cared so much, he'd told her the young man had reminded him of himself at that age. Nassos, who'd gotten little help from his ailing grandfather, had to fish from a row boat and sell his catch at the market to support them. Lys's father, Kristos, also dirt-poor, started fishing with him.

Both men had wanted more out of life and had gone after it. In time they built businesses that grew until Kristos decided to travel to New York and take over a hotel there.

Nassos was able to buy property in Heraklion and build a hotel on Crete. He'd made it into a huge success story. Nassos had seen that same hunger in Takis, who he said was brilliant and had vision in a way that separated him from the masses. Both men wanted Takis to realize his dream. That's why Nassos had made it possible for Takis to travel to New York and work at the hotel Lys's father had owned. Their hunch had paid off in a huge way.

Later on, through Nassos, Lys learned more about the enterprising Takis. His chain of hotels and stock market investments had turned him into a billionaire. She found herself fantasizing about him, and loved Nassos for his goodness. He was a saint who'd become the father she'd lost. Imagine making such a thing possible for the younger man, who was a homegrown Cretan like himself!

Though she couldn't imagine how Takis Manolis would feel when he heard the news that he was the new half owner of the Rodino Hotel, she was excited to be able to carry out Nassos's final wish. In truth she couldn't wait to meet this twenty-nine-year-old man she'd heard talked about for so long.

She'd endowed him with her idea of what the perfect Cretan man looked like. It was very silly of her, but she couldn't help it. Both her father and Nassos had made him out to be someone so unique and fascinating, she'd wouldn't be human if her imagination hadn't taken over.

As for her being the other half owner, she didn't know how she felt about it yet. Everything depended on today's meeting.

It was midmorning as Lys left her hotel in Milan dressed in a heavy black Ralph Lauren shirt dress she could wear without a coat. After setting out on her mission, she gave the limo driver directions to the *castello* outside the city. Then she sat back to take in the fabulous scenery of farms and villas lined with the tall narrow cypress trees indigenous to the region.

Mid-March felt like Heraklion, a cool fifty-eight degrees under cloudy skies. The only difference was that Milan wasn't by the sea. According to Nassos, this refurbished Italian monument built on top of a hill in the thirteen hundreds—originally the home of the first Duc di Lombardi—was a triumph that Takis shared with two business partners. It had become the showplace of Europe.

Lys had come to Italy without letting anyone know where she was going, or why, only that she'd be out of the country for an indefinite period. It was heaven to escape Crete for a little while where few people would recognize her. If anyone knew her reason for coming here, it would make more headlines she didn't want and would do anything to avoid.

Hopefully the press would leave her alone from now on. Though sorrow weighed her down, she intended to ignore any further publicity and carry on as Nassos had expected her to do.

The driver let her out at the base of steps leading to the front entrance. During her climb, she marveled at the trees and flowers surrounding the building. This was a magnificent edifice, high up where she could see the landscape in the far distance. No wonder the Duc di Lombardi found this the perfect place to rule his kingdom.

Inside the entry she was struck by the palatial grandeur with its sweeping corridor of glass doors and chandeliers. The exquisite furniture and paintings of a former time created a matchless tapestry of beauty in the Italian tradition.

A few hotel guests came out of the dining room area. Others walked down the hallway toward the front desk. A lovely woman at the counter, maybe thirty, smiled at her. "May I help you?" she asked in Italian.

Lys answered in English because she could only speak a few words in Italian. "I'm here to see Mr. Manolis, if that's possible."

"Do you have an appointment?" Her switch to excellent English was impressive.

"No. I just flew in to Milan. If he's not available, I'll make an appointment and come back because this is vitally important to me."

"Are you a tour guide?"

"No."

The woman studied her briefly before she said, "What's your name?"

"Ms. Theron."

"If you'll take a seat, I'll see if I can locate him."

Wonderful. He was here somewhere. She'd been prepared to fly to New York to see him if necessary. By coming here first, she'd saved herself a long overseas flight.

This close now to meeting the man her father and Nassos had cared so much about, she felt an attachment to him difficult to explain. Apparently if she'd met this Takis in Heraklion and had started dating him, Nassos would have given his wholehearted approval.

Lys was dying to know what he looked like. As Nassos had explained in his letter to her, he never liked mixing business with his personal life, so she could only guess. Neither he nor Danae had ever mentioned that aspect of him. With a heightened sense of excitement, she turned and sat on one of the beautiful upholstered chairs with the distinctive Duc di Lombardi logo. Her heart pounded hard while she waited to meet Takis.

Midmorning Takis sat with his partners in the private dining room on the second floor of the *castello*. This was the first time he'd had a chance to speak to them after returning from Crete. So far he was no closer to knowing what to do about his worry over his parents and he wanted their opinions. Vincenzo had asked that breakfast be brought up from the kitchen, but Takis had lost his appetite and only wanted coffee.

"You don't have to make any kind of a rash decision right now," his friend counseled. "Rather than just a weekend visit, why don't you simply go back to Tylissos for a couple of weeks? We'll be fine without you. Stay with your family, see what you can do to help out. Surely if there's something wrong with either of your parents, you'll pick up on it and go from there."

As usual, Vincenzo, the present-day Duc di Lombardi, made sense.

Cesare Donati, whose oversight of the restaurant had turned the hotel into *the* place to dine in all of Europe, eyed him over his cup of coffee. "What would be wrong by going home and asking them outright if there's a problem they don't want you to know about? Do it in front of the whole family so if anyone squirms, you'll see it."

That was good advice too. Cesare wasn't one to hold back. He acted on instincts, thus the reason he was the best restaurateur on five continents.

"I'm listening, guys, and am taking both ideas under consideration." Two weeks with his family would give him enough time to get the truth out of them. While he was there he could also track down the woman he'd seen at the funeral whose image wouldn't leave his mind.

While he was deep in thought, his phone rang. Takis checked the caller ID. It was the front desk. He clicked on. "Yes, Sofia?" The woman was Swiss-born and spoke six languages.

"Sorry to bother you when I know you're in a meeting, but a woman I don't recognize has flown to Milan and come to the *castello* to see you. She's not a tour guide and says it's of vital importance, but she didn't explain the nature of her business. She had no card. Her last name is something like Tierrun."

"What's her nationality?"

"She sounds American to me." Maybe she'd been sent from his headquarters in New York for a special reason, but Takis found it strange that his assistant hadn't said anything. "Do you wish to meet with her, or shall I make an appointment?"

Takis had no idea what this was all about, but he might as well take care of it now. "I'll be right there. Take her back to my office." He rang off and glanced at his friends. "I've got to meet someone downstairs. Thanks for the much needed advice. I'll talk to you later."

Lys followed the concierge down a hall lined with several doors. She opened the one on the right. "Mr. Takis will be with you in a minute. Make yourself comfortable. Would you care for coffee or tea while you wait?"

"Nothing, thank you."

After the woman left, Lys sat down near the desk. On the top of it were several little framed snapshots of what she assumed were family photos. Some she surmised were of his parents, some were his siblings and small children. Along with those pictures was a small statue of King Minos, the mythological leader of the great Minoan civilization on Crete, who was clothed in mythology.

As she continued to look around the uncluttered room, a cry escaped her lips. Hanging on the wall across from her was a large framed picture of a younger Nassos with a lot of black hair, standing on the deck of his yacht in a sport shirt and trousers. Takis must have taken it with a camera and had sent the photo to be enlarged. There were no other pictures.

With pounding heart she jumped up from the chair and walked over to get a closer look. Nassos's signature was in the bottom right hand corner. He'd personalized it. *Bravo, Takis.* He signed everything with a flourish.

Seeing him so alive and vital in the picture brought tears to her eyes. He would be thrilled if he knew his autographed photo hung in the office of his unofficial protégé in the most prominent spot. The fact that this man had honored Nassos this way told her a lot about his character and she knew he was deserving of the gift he was about to receive.

Lys heard a little rap on the open door and whirled around.

She hadn't known what she'd expected to see. Only her imagination could have provided that. But it wasn't the tall, hard-muscled male so striking in a rugged way who'd just walked in his office…an olive-complexioned man come to life from ancient Crete though he was dressed in a stone-colored business suit and tie.

"Oh—" she cried softly because the sight of him caused her thoughts to reel.

Those penetrating hazel eyes of his put her in mind of one of those heroic dark-blond warriors depicted in frescos on the walls of temples and museums. She studied his arresting features, remembering one prince who could have been his double. The five o'clock shadow on his firm jaw gave him a sensual appeal she hadn't been prepared for.

While she continued to stare at him, she realized he'd been examining her the way someone did who couldn't believe what he was seeing. He gave her a slight nod. "The woman at the desk thought you were American, but didn't quite get your name." The man spoke English with a heavy accent she found exciting.

"I'm Lys Theron," she said in Greek.

A look of astonishment crossed over his face. "Wait," he said, as if sorting out a puzzle. "Theron… Kristos Theron. He was *your* father?"

"Yes."

Clearly her answer shocked him.

"He was a wonderful man. It came as a terrible blow when I heard about the plane crash. He'd been very kind to me. I'm so sorry you lost him."

"So am I."

The second she'd spoken, silence enveloped the room's interior. His eyes seemed to go dark from some unnamed emotion. A hand went to the back of his neck, as if he were questioning what he'd just heard. "I saw you at Nassos's funeral last weekend," he murmured in Greek.

His admission shook her to the core. "You were there?"

"That's right. I wouldn't have missed it. Aside from my father, Nassos Rodino was the finest man I ever knew. His death came as a great shock to me."

He'd been at the church! No wonder he'd stared so hard at her, but she hadn't seen him. Her pain had been too great.

She took a deep breath. "To know you flew to

Heraklion to honor him, and that you have his photograph hanging in this office, would have meant the world to him."

A strange sound came out of him. "You're a relation of his?"

"I was seventeen when my father died. Nassos was his best friend and became my guardian. He took me back to Crete where I lived with him and his wife."

He shook his head. "I can't credit it. You and I never met, yet your father and Nassos are the reason I have a life here."

"I've heard about you for years and have been wanting to meet you. You're the brilliant son of Nikanor Manolis from Tylissos. Nassos's belief in you was clearly deserved."

His chest rose and fell visibly. "His support was nothing short of a miracle," he whispered.

"A miracle couldn't work if the seeds of greatness weren't already there."

Another unearthly quiet emanated from him, prompting her to speak. "I was sixteen when I first learned about you. Nassos came to visit often and asked my father if he'd give you a job at the hotel in New York. I thought it was so wonderful that they wanted to help you so you could go to college. They really believed in you!"

He moved closer. "Your father's close friendship with Nassos made it possible for me to work and go to school. He was very good to me."

"To me too." She smiled. "It was hard to lose him when I did."

She felt his compassionate gaze. "I can only imagine your feelings right now. I'm sorry you've suffered so many losses."

"Death comes to us all at some point." She sucked in her breath, still dazed by his striking looks, in fact by the whole situation. "To be honest, I've always wanted to meet the famous Takis Manolis. The last time Nassos spoke of you, he said you were already a living legend before you were thirty."

His dark brows furrowed as if in utter disbelief over those words, revealing a humility she found admirable.

"Please. Sit down." While she did his bidding, he paced the floor looking shaken, then he stopped. "Can I get you anything? Have you had breakfast?"

"Thank you, but I ate before I left the hotel in Milan several hours ago. I should have contacted you for an appointment ahead of time, but decided to take my chances and fly here first. I haven't taken a real trip in a long time. I love getting away from everything for a little while."

"I don't blame you. I saw what was written about you in the paper while I was in Crete. The press manages to find a way if they're looking for a story." By the tone of disgust in his voice, she imagined he'd had to deal with his share of unwanted invasions. She could relate to his feelings, making it easier to confide in him.

"Nassos's unexplained, unexpected death wasn't solved until a week ago when the medical examiner said he'd died from a subarachnoid hemorrhage. Over the last month while everything was up in the air, the press labeled me everything from a murderer who'd poisoned him, to an opportunistic floozy. You could add adulteress, narcissistic liar and evil spawn of Satan in some of the more sordid tabloids. The list goes on and on."

Their eyes met. "Is that all?" he teased unexpectedly, catching her off guard. His bone-melting charm, not to mention his refreshing humor was so welcome, she felt a great release and laughter bubbled out of her.

She could easily understand why Nassos had found him an extraordinary human being in ways other than his business acumen. After reading Nassos's letter, she knew Nassos hadn't talked to him about her or Danae. Nassos had always been a very private person.

"I came to see you for a very specific reason, but if this isn't a good time to talk, please say so. I can return to Milan and wait until I hear from you. Or I'll fly back to Crete and come another time when it's more convenient."

His eyes narrowed on her features. "The daughter whom Nassos helped raise for his best friend has my full, undivided attention. Tell me what's on your mind. Obviously it's very important to you, otherwise you wouldn't have flown all this distance during your bereavement. I'd do anything for him, so that translates I'd do anything for you. Just name it."

Lys felt his sincerity sink deep into her psyche. "Thank you for saying that. I guess I don't have to tell you what this means to me."

Takis sat on the corner of his desk. "How can I help you?" he asked in a quiet tone, drawing her attention to his powerful legs beneath his trousers. She couldn't stop noticing every exciting male trait about him.

"It concerns the hotel in Heraklion."

One of his brows lifted in query. "Go on."

She got up from the chair, struggling with how to approach him. "In his will, every possession and asset of his *except* the hotel was left to his ex-wife, Danae."

The man listening to her didn't move a muscle, but she saw a quickening in his eyes, not knowing what it meant.

"That was as it should be," she continued. "Danae was his devoted wife for twenty-four years. When they divorced, he left her with everything she would need. Now that she has received the full inheritance he left her, I know she'll be well provided for all of her life."

"So I'm presuming the hotel is now yours."

Lys shook her head. "I only have half ownership and didn't want the half he left me."

Lines marred his features before he got to his feet. "That's very strange, but what does any of it have to do with me?" Confusion was written all over his handsome face.

Lys had tried to present this the right way, but she wasn't getting through to him. Taking a deep breath, she said, "Nassos hoped to leave a lasting legacy. Since none of us knows when we're going to die, he took precautions early to preserve that legacy when the time came, whenever that was."

"I still can't believe he's gone." His mournful comment touched her heart.

"Neither can I. Because he didn't have children, it meant putting the hotel in the hands of someone who understands and shares his vision."

Takis was listening. "That was you."

She took a deep breath. "I worked for him, yes. But I think this decision was made because he'd been my guardian and was always protective of me. He probably felt I needed someone to share the responsibility so I wouldn't make a serious mistake."

His brows dipped. "Mistake?"

"Yes. He loved the myth of King Minos, who forgot to rule wisely. Because of his mistake, he was killed by the daughters of King Cocalus, who poured boiling water over him while he was taking a bath. I notice you have a little statue of him."

"The story of King Minos intrigued me as a youth too."

Lys smiled sadly. "It proves you and Nassos had minds that thought alike. More than ever I'm convinced there was only one other person he could think of who would honor what he'd built."

She opened her handbag and pulled out the sealed envelope she handed to him. "That person is you, Kyrie Manolis. His attorney instructed me to give this to you. Any explanations are inside. I don't know the contents."

If Nassos had another flaw besides his pride, it was his secrecy, which had left Lys at a loss.

After clearing her throat she said, "In case you're not aware, it made Nassos happier than you could ever imagine to know that the little help he gave you in the beginning was the only thing you needed to go all the way. It means a lot to me to have met you after all this time. Not everyone could accomplish what you've done in so short a time. I'm truly impressed."

She moved to the door while he stood there in a trancelike state. "I have to get back to Crete. Please don't take long to let me know your plans. I wrote my private cell phone number on the back of that envelope. I live at the hotel and will meet with you at your convenience. Now I must get going. My limo is waiting in the front courtyard. *Kalimera.*"

She hurried down the hall. To stay in that room with him any longer wasn't a good idea. They'd only just met, yet she'd felt a strong, immediate attraction to Takis that had rocked her world. It had gotten its start in the long-ago conversations between her father and Nassos, and the impression she'd created of the younger man who'd been hungry to better his life.

She knew she had to get away from him and leave the *castello* before she didn't want to leave. Lys had never felt these kinds of initial feelings about any man in her life.

Those playboys who'd passed in and out of her life couldn't touch this extraordinary man, who'd earned the highest praise from her father and Nassos. The intense way he was looking at her, the emotions he'd aroused, had caused her bones to melt.

CHAPTER THREE

TAKIS KNEW HE HADN'T dreamed up this meeting with the woman Nassos had helped raise. When she left his office, her flowery fragrance lingered, providing proof she'd been in here.

He'd seen tears in her eyes when she'd heard him enter the room. She'd just been looking at Nassos's picture. The exquisite woman who'd walked down the aisle at the funeral had been his ward at one time. Shame on Takis for wondering if she could have been the mistress talked about in the news.

How old was Lys Theron? Twenty-five, twenty-six? And now she was half owner of the hotel, with Takis owning the other half.

Several emotions bombarded him, not the least of which was the attraction to her he'd felt at the funeral. He looked at the envelope his hand had squeezed without his being aware of it. According to her, this was Nassos's gift to him.

Utterly incredulous, he opened it and pulled out a letter and a deed. To his shock it was official all right, signed with Nassos's distinctive signature, stamped and dated. There it was in bold letters.

Takis Manolis, half owner of the Rodino Hotel in Heraklion.

The letter indicated he should get in touch with the attorney Xander as soon as possible. Once Takis returned to Heraklion, he could sign the deed in front of witnesses so it could be recorded and filed for the court.

He read more. Neither owner would be free to do what they wanted with the hotel until six months had passed.

Aghast, he shook his head. What on earth had possessed Nassos to do such a thing?

Once Takis's hotels in New York had started making money, he'd paid the older hotelier for the help he'd given him. No amount could really be enough. How did you assign goodness a monetary value? He'd tried, but to his chagrin Nassos was now gone and there'd be no last time to thank him for everything.

This unimaginable development had thrown him.

For Nassos to turn around and simply give him half the hotel in Heraklion made no sense whatsoever. Takis didn't want the hotel! He'd paid him back generously.

What in the hell was Nassos thinking? Now that he'd passed away, there was no way to confront him about this. The inconceivable gesture made him feel as if he'd always be the boy who'd come from near poverty. The thought hurt him in a way that went soul deep.

To add to the hurt, this deed had been delivered by special messenger in the form of Nassos's beautiful former ward. Why would he force Takis's hand by making him a co-owner with her?

She was *too* damn beautiful. The kind of woman he never imagined to meet. Didn't want to meet. Only one other woman had touched his heart and she'd died. He didn't want to experience those kinds of feelings again. Yet a few minutes with this woman and a fire had been lit.

How did *she* feel about being half owner with a stranger, even if she knew a lot about him from Nassos and her father?

His thoughts centered on what she'd told him about the way the press had labeled her in the cruelest of ways. With her kind of unforgettable looks, she was an easy target. Was Nassos's divorce the result of his taking on Kristos's lovely teenage daughter to raise?

What business is it of yours to care, Manolis?

Unfortunately it *was* his business until he could fly to Crete and clear up this whole mess with the attorney of record.

Adrenaline surged through his veins. He wished to hell none of this had happened. He still couldn't believe Nassos was gone. Worse, he didn't want to know anything about *her*. Takis wished he'd never laid eyes on her. He didn't want this kind of a complication in his life. Loving a woman made you vulnerable.

A violent epithet flew from his lips. In his rage he tossed the deed across the room. It hit Cesare in the chest as he walked inside Takis's office.

With great calm his friend picked it up and put it on the desk. He shot Takis a questioning glance. "I take it this had something to do with the drop-dead-gorgeous woman I saw leaving the hotel a minute ago. Where on earth did *she* come from?"

Takis had trouble getting his emotions under control. "You don't want to know."

"Yes I do. You've been with several women over the years, but I've never seen you turned inside out by one before."

"It's not just the woman. It's everything!" His voice shook. "I feel like my world has been blown to smithereens and I don't know where I am anymore."

Takis should never have left his parents' home. He should have stayed on Crete and worked alongside his brother. He'd been so certain he'd had all the answers to help his family. But in the end he'd accepted the help of a wealthy man.

The thought of the deeded gift sickened him. That kind of gift might be given to a son, but Takis hadn't been Nassos's son. He was the son of Nikanor, who after all these years still didn't want his money. Neither did his brother. Worse, one of his parents was probably ill and Takis didn't have a clue because he'd been living out of the country for years. He was the ingrate of all time.

"What's the point of anything, Cesare?"

Worry lines darkened the features of his Italian friend. "Hold on, Takis. Come with me. We're going for a ride. My car is parked in the rear lot of the *castello*."

"You don't want to be with me."

"Well, I refuse to leave you here alone. It wouldn't do for Sofia to find you in this condition." Cesare was right about that. He didn't want his assistant privy to his personal life. "Whatever trouble you're in, we're going to talk about it. Let's go."

Takis grabbed the papers and stuffed them inside his suit jacket. They walked swiftly through the corridors past some of the guests to the outside. Cesare started up his sports car. He followed the road around from the back of the *castello* and they drove down the hill to the little village of Sopri. Before long he parked in front of a sports bar on the outskirts that didn't look crowded this time of day.

They went inside and found a quiet spot in a corner. Cesare ordered appetizers and their favorite Peroni, a pale lager from the brewery that had been founded in Lombardi. Once they'd been served rolls along with a hot plate of *grigliata mista di carne,* he eyed Takis.

"You didn't eat breakfast, which might explain the state you were in. You need lunch, *amico*, and you've got me for an audience. Now start talking and don't stop."

Cesare knew Takis's weakness for their grilled sausage, lamb and steak mix. Combined with the lager, it did taste good and he could feel his strength returning.

He pulled the deed out of his pocket and pushed it toward Cesare. "As you know, I attended Nassos Rodino's funeral while I was in Crete. Would you believe in his will he gave half the Hotel Rodino in Heraklion to me as a gift? The other half was given to that woman you saw. She was the courier who delivered it."

His friend studied it. "Who is she?"

"Lys Theron, the daughter of Kristos Theron, the

hotel owner in New York who gave me my first job after I reached the States. You remember me talking about him. When he died, his best friend, Nassos, Rodino became her guardian and brought her back to Crete to raise."

A low whistle came out of Cesare. But Takis didn't want to talk about the beautiful woman who'd robbed him of breath the moment he'd laid eyes on her. She was another problem altogether.

"I thought the money I sent to Nassos for his help had changed his image of me as the poverty-stricken teen from Tylissos." He swallowed part of his lager. "But I was wrong. In his mind's eye I would always be the poor son of poor Nikanor Manolis, humbly scraping out a living day after day.

"I never wanted anything from Nassos. His kindness gave me a new life, but I paid him back. To be handed a deed to part ownership of a property that isn't mine, that I never earned, is worse than a stiletto to the gut."

Cesare shot forward in his seat. "You couldn't be more wrong. It's his tribute to your raving success."

"You think?"

"Of course."

Takis shook his head. "Maybe the problem lies inside me. Maybe I've been too proud wanting to make a success of my life. Nassos's gift of the hotel takes me back to the time when I was eighteen. He approached me about furthering my education, not the other way around, Cesare.

"The hotel manager I worked for arranged for me to meet Nassos. I never asked for his help. When I finally accepted it and left for New York, I started paying him back as soon as I could. But being given half ownership of his hotel now doesn't feel right and has made me feel…guilty all over again."

"What's gotten into you, Takis? Guilty for what? Help me understand."

"That I've failed my family."

"In what way?"

"I left them to do something purely selfish. I accepted a rich man's help. My father couldn't give me that kind of help or encourage me. If I'd been any kind of a man, I would have stayed home and helped him."

"That's crazy talk, Takis. I left home too in order to pursue a dream and accepted a lot of help along the way."

"This is different, Cesare. You're not a Cretan."

"So what? I'm a Sicilian. What's the difference? My pride is no less fierce than yours."

Takis had no answer for that. "You don't understand. My brother stayed behind to work with my father. He never failed him. But that wasn't the case with his second-born son. What did I do? I took off. When I think about it now, I cringe to realize how deeply I must have disgraced him."

"Disgraced?" Cesare sounded angry. "You don't know any such thing. He must be bursting with pride over you. When was the last time you had a real heart-to-heart talk with him?"

"Before I left for New York, we talked. I went to him with ideas for what we could do with the hotel. He looked me in the eye and told me my plans for the family hotel didn't fit his vision, and that one day when I was a man, I'd understand. That was it! End of conversation. It shut me down. After eleven years I'm afraid I still don't understand."

"Then you need to force another conversation with him and find out what he meant."

"My father isn't easy to talk to."

"Then it's time you faced him so you won't stay in that hellhole you're digging for yourself. Let me ask you a question. Do you think *me* selfish? Or Vincenzo?"

Takis didn't have to voice the easy *no* that came to his mind.

"Come on and finish your food. Then we're going back to the *castello* to talk to Vincenzo before he leaves for Lake Como with Gemma. You're not the only one who has known the pain of separation from family. Don't forget that he *ran* from his father as fast as he could and hid out in New York under a different name for over ten years."

Takis had forgotten nothing. The three of them would never have met if they hadn't left their homes and their countries and gone to New York. He couldn't imagine what his life would have been like if he hadn't met Cesare and Vincenzo. The friendship they'd forged in college had changed his entire world.

All because Nassos made it possible for you, Manolis, said a voice in his head, sending him into worse turmoil.

Cesare paid the bill and got to his feet. "Are you ready?"

Once Lys had received the return phone call from Danae at noon, she walked out the door of the penthouse foyer to the elevator off the small hallway to await her arrival. The penthouse in Crete had been Nassos's domain, and a decision had to be made about the furnishings.

After being back a week from Milan, Lys still hadn't heard a word from Takis Manolis. But she'd daydreamed about him and what it would be like to go out with him. Since meeting him, she couldn't imagine ever being attracted to another man. She'd hoped to know his plans before telling Danae the latest state of affairs, but no such luck.

The doors of the elevator opened. Lys greeted the dark-haired beauty and walked back in the penthouse with her. Dressed in mourning clothes, she looked particularly elegant in a Kasper color-blocked black Jacquard jacket and skirt. Danae had always been a fashion plate and was the true love of Nassos's life.

No matter what he'd told Lys in his letter to her, she feared Danae might still blame her for their divorce. The pain of that would never leave her. No olive branch offered could ever change the past.

If Lys had known what would happen after Nassos had insisted she leave New York and come to live with him and Danae, she would have run away rather than have stepped foot on Crete. Hindsight was a wonderful thing, but it came far too late.

"Thank you for coming, Danae. I'm sure you hoped we'd seen the last of each other at the funeral, but I'm carrying out one last thing Nassos would have wanted done, even if it wasn't in the will. Come in the living room and sit down—I'd like to explain a few things."

The older woman followed her and found a seat on one of the upholstered chairs. Danae's natural olive complexion had paled. "I can't imagine what would have been so important you had to see me in person."

"Maybe you'll think it isn't important when I tell you, but I have to do it. As you know, Nassos left me half the hotel and nothing else. That means everything in this penthouse is yours. He lived up here after he left the villa. I happen to know you are the one who designed it and put it all together years ago. You're a real artist in many ways. All this furniture you picked out, the paintings... You know he would have wanted you to have everything."

She jumped to her feet, visibly disturbed. "I don't want anything," she bit out too fast, revealing her pain.

Lys could understand that and her heart went out to her. "If you don't want any of it, then you need to make arrangements for it to be sold or given away, or whatever you think is best. Otherwise I'll ask the co-owner of the hotel to do with it as he or she wishes."

"Who is it?"

"Would it surprise you to know its Takis Manolis?"

Danae's head reared. "Actually it doesn't. Nassos liked him very much."

Lys was glad she'd told her the truth. "I don't know if he wants it. But until he signs and files the official document with the court, it's still up in the air. On Xander's instructions I flew to Italy, handed him the documents and left."

"So you met him."

"Yes."

"What's he like?"

She took a deep breath. "Very attractive, but I haven't heard from him. Maybe he's trying to find a way to get out of it and possibly designate a person from his New York chain. That could be the reason there's been no word yet.

"Xander will have to be the one to keep us informed. I just thought you might like to have the movers come before anything else happens."

No sound came out of Danae. Lys could tell she was in a bad way and she wanted to comfort her.

"Nassos's death came as a painful shock to both of us." The anguished look on Danae's face prompted Lys to reveal something she'd held back since the divorce. "I'd like to talk frankly with you. When my father died, I was afraid to come to Crete, where I didn't know anyone. But I was underage and as you know, Nassos made a promise to my father to take care of me in case he died. I realize that my arrival was probably your worst nightmare, but it was something I had no control over."

Danae lowered her eyes.

"You were so wonderful to me, I got over a lot of my pain and started to be happy with you. In time I learned to adore you. But you must know that *you* were the great passion of Nassos's life."

The other woman started to tremble.

"I have something to show you." Lys pulled the letter from Nassos out of her purse and handed it to her. Nassos hadn't meant anyone else to read it, but Lys couldn't keep it from Danae, who deserved to know the truth.

"So you won't think I'm holding anything back, I want you to read this. Xander gave it to me after reading the contents of the will to you."

She watched as the older woman took in the contents. Soon her shoulders shook.

"As you've read, Nassos wanted children and I happened to fill a hole in his heart for a while as the daughter you two never had."

Danae looked crushed and put a hand to her throat. "I—I was afraid I wouldn't be able to love a child that wasn't mine. That's why I didn't want to adopt."

"I can understand that. I'm sure a lot of childless parents worry about the same thing when they adopt. But you showed me so much love, perhaps it was just that Nassos had more faith in your parenting abilities than you did. When he moved to the penthouse after your divorce, he was a ruined man."

"Why didn't he tell me all these things?" she cried in agony.

"His pride. What about yours? Would you have listened?"

She shook her dark head. "I don't know. I don't know. I harbored a lot of resentment over the years because he didn't want me to work. When he begged me to consider adoption, I felt anger because of the many times I'd begged him to let me try even part-time work. We were both so hardheaded."

"I'm so sorry, Danae." As they stared at each other, Lys reached for the letter she put back in her purse. "I hope you'll listen to me now because there's something else I've wanted to tell you since your separation from him." Her throat swelled with emotion.

"I love you. You were kind and loving and helped me so much. The two of you had a beautiful marriage in so many ways. For what it's worth, you would have made a wonderful mother. Maybe there's a man out there who could fulfill that dream for you. Many women have babies at your age. It's not too late if you decide to get married again. You're a very beautiful woman."

A long silence ensued before Danae jumped up from the chair and hugged her hard. "Thank you for saying that to me. I love you too, Lys. You have no idea how much I've missed you."

With those words, Lys's pain was lifted. "I feel the same." She finally let go of Danae, and wiped her eyes. "Tell me something else. Would you have liked to inherit the hotel and run it?"

Danae shook her head. "It doesn't matter what I would have liked. He wanted a stay-at-home wife and didn't want me working at the hotel after we were married. Now I'm not interested."

"But you could read between the lines in his letter to me. He admitted he was wrong about divorcing you, and he was wrong not to have let you work alongside him after you were married."

She grasped Lys's hands. "You're very sweet, but it's too late for that."

"Are you sure? You could talk to Xander and fight for it. I'd step aside in an instant if I knew it was what you wanted."

"It isn't. Truly. But I'll take your advice and get movers in here to ship everything back to the villa."

"I'm glad about that!" Lys hugged her again, then headed for the foyer.

Danae followed. "Where are you going?"

"Back to my room. I need to return Anita's call. You remember my mother's friend? She came to Nassos's funeral."

"Of course. It was wonderful of her to come."

"I know. I couldn't believe she'd fly all this way from New York." Lys pressed the button that opened the elevator doors, then turned to Danae. "If you need anything, just phone me."

"I want you to come to the villa as soon as you can. It's so empty now."

"I promise to visit you all the time."

"You mean it?"

"Of course I do. I love you, Danae. *Yassou.*"

Lys rode the private elevator six floors to the lobby, then took the main elevator back to the third floor. She needed to make a phone call to Anita on Long Island. They'd stayed in close touch over the years.

Anita had invited Lys to stay with her and her husband, Bob, for a time. Maybe a little vacation would be a good thing. Maybe not. She just didn't know.

The limo pulled up to the Rodino Hotel in Heraklion. For the moment he had business to take care of here. Lys Theron had no idea he'd flown to Heraklion two days ago to stay with his family. Now he was ready to talk to her, but he wanted the element of surprise on his side.

Before he'd left for New York, Takis had done every job there was to do there at the hotel for that year. He'd often escorted VIPs to the penthouse Nassos used for business. No doubt Lys Theron lived there now.

There was a private elevator down the right hall that went straight to the top. If Nassos hadn't changed his six-digit birthday code on the keypad, Takis would be able to go on up. Otherwise he'd have to phone her from downstairs. His pulse raced at the thought of seeing her again.

The code hadn't changed. After the doors opened, he stepped inside for the short ride and entered the outer hallway when it stopped. But he needed to alert her he was here. Even if it was presumptuous, when he explained how he'd gained access to the elevator, he hoped she'd understand.

Takis had just pressed the digits of the phone number written on the envelope she'd given him when the door to the penthouse opened. He received a surprise because instead of Lys Theron standing there, the stylish black-haired woman he'd seen at the older man's funeral emerged without her veil.

She glared at him. "No one is permitted up here. Who are you?"

"I'm sorry to have alarmed you," he murmured. "I was just calling Kyria Theron to let her know I was out here."

The attractive woman scrutinized him. "This isn't her apartment."

What?

"How did you get up here?"

Takis would have to proceed carefully. "I'm the new co-owner of the hotel." After many talks with his partners in the last week, that's what he was saying right now, but it was subject to change depending on many things.

"What's your name?" she murmured.

"Takis Manolis."

Her eyes widened. "Lys told me."

He nodded. "I saw you at the church on the day of

Nassos's funeral." This had to be the widow. "You must be Kyria Rodino."

"Yes. I was married to Nassos for twenty-four years and heard your name mentioned with fondness for the last twelve of them."

The revelation stunned him. "He was instrumental in changing my life. I'll never forget him."

Her eyes glistened over. "Neither will I."

Takis had a hard time taking it all in. "I'm very sorry for your loss. Please forgive me. I thought Kyria Theron lived here. Do you know where I can find her?"

"She has her own suite at the hotel. I have to leave and will ride down in the elevator with you."

Takis had made a big mistake coming up here.

Once they reached the hotel foyer, he thanked her for her help and the two of them parted company. He walked into the main lounge where he could be private and rang her number.

Before long he heard, "Kyrie Manolis?" She sounded surprised. "I wondered when I might hear from you."

"I just arrived at the hotel and am in the lounge. We have to talk." Before any more time passed he needed to explain that he'd trespassed earlier and had alarmed Nassos's former wife. "When will it be convenient for you?"

"I'll be right down."

"Efharisto."

Within two minutes the dark-blonde woman he'd come to see walked toward him dressed in a storm-gray crewneck sweater with long sleeves and a matching skirt. Some Cretan women in mourning wore darker clothes, if not black, for a long time.

Yet even garbed in somber colors, the feminine curves of her figure and the long legs he admired couldn't be hidden. She not only ignited his senses, but those of every male within her radius.

Takis had the additional advantage of being able to stare into those violet eyes at close range. When he'd been inside the church, he'd thought no eyes could be that color. At the time he'd assumed the sun shining through the stained glass had to have been responsible.

But the hotel lounge was no church. If anything, their color bordered on purple and mesmerized him almost as much as the enticing curve of her mouth. He wondered how many men had known its taste and had run their hands through hair as luscious as swirling caramel cream.

"It's nice to see you again, Kyrie Manolis."

"I've been looking forward to talking to you too. Since we're co-owners, I'd rather you called me Takis."

"So you've decided."

"Yes. Do you mind if I call you Lys?"

"I'd prefer it. If you'll come with me, we'll go to my suite to talk. Until the situation is settled and made official, I'd prefer us to meet in private rather than Nassos's office so we don't have to make explanations to anyone."

"You took the words out of my mouth."

They walked to the bank of elevators and took the next empty one that carried them to the third floor. He followed her to the end of the hall where she opened the door to a small foyer. It led into a typical hotel suite sitting room. Nothing special here, nothing that told him about her personality.

"There's a guest bathroom down that hall. If you'd like to freshen up, I'll call the kitchen and ask for lunch to be served. Anything special you would like?"

"Why don't you surprise me?" He watched her disappear before he left the room. When he returned, he found her seated in one of the chairs around the coffee table with the phone in her hand.

Her gaze wandered over him as he sat down. He enjoyed the sensation far too much and castigated himself. "Danae just called to tell me she met you outside the penthouse door looking for me. I'm curious. How *did* you gain access to the private elevator?"

He leaned forward with his hands clasped between this legs. "When I worked here for a year, I was given the code to take VIPs to the penthouse for Nassos."

A genuine smile broke out on her beautiful face. "You knew his birthday code."

"I'm afraid I couldn't resist finding out if it still worked, but I caught Kyria Rodino off guard. For that, I'm sorry."

"That's my fault. When I told you I lived at the hotel, I failed to be more specific. It wasn't until Nassos separated from Danae that he moved to the penthouse."

"I had no right to do what I did."

"I'm sure Danae was more amused than offended once you introduced yourself. It's something Nassos might have pulled if he'd been in your shoes. He had an impish side and indicated you were clever."

"If you translate that, it means I went where angels feared to tread far too often." The gentle chuckle that came out of her coincided with the rap on the door to the suite. Takis got up first. "I'll get it."

After tipping the employee, he carried their tray of food into the sitting room and put it on the coffee table. He removed the covers on *horiatiki* salad and Greek club sandwiches filled with lamb while she poured the coffee for them.

They both sat back to eat. She appeared hungry too. He swallowed his second half in no time. "This is an excellent lunch. Kudos to the chef."

"You can tell Eduardo yourself."

Takis glanced at her over his coffee cup. "My attorney examined the legal work and it is quite clear that Nassos didn't give either of us a choice. We're stuck for six months. How do you feel about that?"

She averted her eyes. "I don't have a right to feel much of anything. As I told you earlier, it's possible he didn't want me to be the sole owner for fear I might make bad decisions. The one man he felt he could trust was you, so I can understand why he made certain you would be there to help me if I got into trouble."

Nice as that compliment sounded, he didn't buy it. "*Have* you gotten into trouble in the past?"

His question seemed to unsettle her. She put her coffee cup on the table. "Not in business, but he didn't always approve of the men I've dated."

That had been the one thing on his mind since he'd

seen her in the church. If she was in a relationship now, he should be happy about it.

No doubt Nassos hadn't liked any male who tried to get too close to her. He'd probably had a man in mind for her, but only when the time was right. By becoming her guardian, he'd taken his responsibility seriously.

"Though I can't imagine it, is it possible he didn't want you to fall for someone who wanted more than your love?" A man would have to be blind not to want a relationship with her if he could. The fact that she was the owner of one of the most famous hotels in Greece would make a man heady if he could have both.

She sat back in the chair. "He couldn't have known that he would die this early in his life."

"No," he muttered. "No man knows that."

"But I wouldn't put it past him to have worried that I might make a bad emotional decision because of some man, even at the age of sixty or seventy."

"If Nassos had a fear that you could put the welfare of the hotel at risk no matter your age, he would never have willed half of it to you. I'm convinced your personal happiness was all that concerned him."

"Coming from you, that means a lot."

What Takis still hadn't worked out yet was why Nassos had made *him* co-owner. His partners had tried to disabuse him of the notion that when Nassos had made out his will, he'd seen Takis as the needy boy from Crete.

He still didn't want his father to know he'd inherited it from Nassos. He feared his parent wouldn't understand and would wonder what Takis had done to deserve such a gift.

Her features grew animated and she got to her feet to pour herself another cup of coffee. "Now that you're here, I have a proposition for you."

The course of their conversation intrigued him. "Go ahead."

"When six months have passed, Nassos said we could do whatever we wanted with the hotel. I'll be honest and tell you up front that I'd like to buy your half. I'll be twenty-seven by then and will have come into the inheritance from my father. Whatever price you set, I'll be able to meet it."

Takis hadn't been expecting a proposition like that. Her own father's inheritance would make her independently wealthy. There was no question she'd be able to buy him out. In half a year's time this unwanted situation could be turned around and he'd be done with it.

"On the face of it I like the idea. Since you worked with Nassos, then he would have taught you how to invest your money wisely."

Her eyes lit up, reaching his insides. "I'd like to think that's true. Takis...if it suits you, I'll continue to run the hotel, leaving you free to go back to your other businesses." If she was eager to see the last of him, he had news for her. "But if you want to be here full-time in a hands-on capacity to honor Nassos's wishes, then we'll work things out any way you'd like."

Hands-on?

Not only was she gorgeous, she was too good to be true. He hadn't known what to expect, but it wasn't this amenable woman whose only agenda he could see was to eventually own the hotel outright. If she had an ulterior motive somewhere, he hadn't detected it yet.

When she'd told him at the *castello* they were co-owners, hadn't Takis wanted to be free of Nassos's gift?

He got to his feet, troubled because she was seducing him without even trying. Not since losing his girlfriend had he felt such emotion. But this was much stronger because he was no longer an eighteen-year-old boy.

"You've made this insanely easy for me in every way. Why don't we meet tomorrow morning at the Villa Kerasia outside the city? The quiet, small back room of the dining area will help us to keep a low profile while we talk business and discuss where we go from here."

"That sounds good to me," she answered without taking a breath. "Before you leave, I wanted you to know that within the week the penthouse will be empty. You can use it, decorate it, do whatever you want."

"Thank you. But when I'm in Crete, I stay with my family."

Her eyes went suspiciously bright. "Of course. Tylissos isn't that far from here. How lucky you are to have family to come home to. I envy you."

"I *am* fortunate," he admitted, but his thoughts were on her. She'd just lost Nassos and would be vulnerable for a long time. Takis didn't want to feel any emotions where she was concerned, but to his chagrin she'd aroused much more in him than the urge to comfort her. "Thank you for lunch. I'll let myself out and see you in the morning. How does eight thirty sound to you?"

"Perfect."

So was she. Tomorrow he'd be with her again. It was the only reason he could leave the hotel at all.

CHAPTER FOUR

LYS AWAKENED EARLY the next morning. She'd been restless during the night, otherwise her comforter wouldn't be on the floor at the side of her bed. The unexpected advent of Takis Manolis in her life had shaken her world.

The fact that he would be co-owner of the hotel with her for the next six months wasn't nearly as disconcerting as the man himself. He was a Cretan Adonis who'd gotten under her skin and had turned her insides to mush the first time she'd laid eyes on him. She wished to heaven she weren't excited to be meeting him for breakfast, but she couldn't turn off those hormones working madly inside her body.

There was nothing professional about her feelings for him. She had no idea how she was going to be able to work with him and not reveal how susceptible she was to his male charisma. No woman alive could be indifferent to him. Somehow she needed to be the exception. But she feared that it would be an impossible task.

Once she'd showered and washed her hair, Lys changed her mind five times about what to wear, something she never did, which proved he was in her head. She eventually settled on pleated navy pants with a navy blouse edged in navy lace and matching sweater.

Not only would she continue to wear dark colors to honor Nassos's memory, but she refused to dress in order to attract Takis's attention. Other women probably did it on a regular basis. But his appeal had affected her so greatly, it was embarrassing. She had no idea how long Danae would wear black before returning to her normal wardrobe. Lys would follow her example.

Once she'd brushed her hair and put on a soft pink lipstick, she left the hotel driving one of their service vans so she wouldn't be recognized by the paparazzi. She headed out of town under an overcast sky to the little settlement of Vlahiana southwest of Heraklion. She took in the beauty of the hills and vineyards rolling in the distance. Several villages clung to the hillsides, beckoning her toward them.

Takis had lived on Crete until he was eighteen and probably knew every inch of it. She was pleased he'd wanted them to meet at the small country inn hidden away where there wouldn't be any press around.

Nassos had once brought her and Danae here, explaining about the building that had been completely restored with ancient stones, a perfect blend with the near-white bleached wood. The artist in him had liked what had been done to it. She didn't wonder that Takis had chosen this same place to talk.

To her surprise, she saw his tall, well-honed physique walking toward her as she pulled up in the small parking area. He could have no way of knowing what she'd worn, but he'd dressed in charcoal-colored trousers and a navy sport shirt open at the neck, looking marvelous.

"We match," he said after opening the van door for her. As she got out, the scent of the soap he'd used in the shower assailed her senses. Her arm brushed against his chest by accident. The slight contact sent a thrill of excitement through her body. "I've already ordered our breakfast. It's waiting out on the back patio for us."

It turned out they had the area to themselves. The trellis roof above them dripped with shocking red bougainvillea. He helped her to sit at the small round table before he took a seat opposite her. The sight of so many delicious-looking items told her he was a typical Cretan who loved his food. There were sausages, smoked pork, eggs with *staka*, cream cheese pie and coffee.

She bit into a piece of pie. "If I ate this way every morning, pretty soon I wouldn't be able to get through the doors to the office."

"That will never be your problem, and I happen to think it's much nicer to eat while we talk business."

"I won't argue with you there." Her awareness of him made it difficult to keep her eyes off him while he devoured his food.

As he drank his coffee, he asked, "Were you running the hotel singlehandedly before Nassos died?"

"Pretty much, along with the general manager. Nassos spent most of his time watching over his other investments, which are now Danae's. But there's no question Nassos kept his eagle eye on everything. Since he's been gone, I've continued to do things the same way, but I'll admit I worry that I'm missing something."

"Do the staff know you're the new owner?"

"No. I'm sure they think that Nassos gave the hotel to Danae even though he divorced her. I know the manager assumes as much."

His piercing gaze stared directly into hers. "How do you feel about having to share the business with me?"

She sat back in the chair. "To be honest, when the attorney gave me Nassos's letter and I read what was inside, I almost went into shock. But by the time I flew to Italy, I'd managed to calm down."

"Your anger didn't show."

"I never felt anger. Not at all. If anything I felt hurt for Danae, who should have inherited the hotel. They met years ago while she'd been working at another hotel. She would be a natural to run everything, but he was too blind to see what he was doing."

He lowered his coffee cup. "You didn't expect to inherit?"

She frowned. "I didn't expect him to die, but I know what you meant to say. I had no expectations. I imagined that in time I'd meet a man, get married and years from now lose Nassos. Instead, he's gone and he has made you co-owner. That's all I know. But to answer your question, no, I'm not angry."

"What did you mean he was too blind?"

Lys shouldn't have said what she did. Now he'd dig until he got the answer he wanted. At this point it didn't matter if he knew the truth. In fact it would be better if it did.

"Tell you what. If you've finished eating, why don't we go to the hotel?" She was enjoying this time with him far too much. "If I show you the letter Nassos instructed the attorney to give to me, then you'll understand and won't have so many questions. I wish I had brought it with me. Did you bring a car?"

"No. I came in a taxi from home."

"Then I'll drive us back to town and we can talk in my sitting room at the hotel. Would it bother you if I'm behind the wheel?"

His half smile gave her a fluttery feeling in her chest. "I'm looking forward to it." He put some bills on the table before helping her up. It had been a long time since she'd been with a man, let alone have one to help her into the van.

The thrill of being with him was like nothing she'd ever experienced. She wished they were going off and not coming back. A silly thought, but one that told her she was in serious trouble where Takis was concerned.

Before long she pulled into the private parking space in the hotel garage and they rode the elevator to her floor. They'd done this before when she'd welcomed him inside her room. After telling him he was welcome to freshen up, she went into the bedroom to get the letter out of the side table drawer.

Once she'd made a detour to her own bathroom, she entered the sitting room and handed it to him before subsiding in one of the upholstered chairs around the coffee table. She'd never invited a man into her hotel room before. But with Takis, everything was feeling so natural.

Takis felt her eyes on him as he opened it to read. Within seconds he couldn't believe what Nassos had written to her. Near the end of it came the part where Takis's name was mentioned.

> Before you take possession, you must give the sealed envelope to Takis Manolis. You've heard me and Danae talk about him often enough. When he came to Crete periodically, we'd discuss business on my yacht, where we could be private.
>
> You'll know where to find him when the time comes. The two of you will share ownership for six months. After that time period, you'll both be free to make any decisions you want.
>
> By the time you read this, he's probably married with children and grandchildren too. I've thought of him as the son I never had.

The son Nassos never had?

"What's wrong, Takis? You've gone pale."

He must have read the whole letter half a dozen times before he realized he wasn't alone in the room. His head swung around. Takis had gotten it all wrong. He could throw the idea of pity out the window. Nassos *had* looked at him as a son. More than that, he'd looked on Lysette, his French nickname for her, as his daughter.

This letter explaining the reason for the Rodino divorce helped him understand why Lys had been hurt for Danae's sake. It showed his love for Lys and hinted of the affection and regard Nassos had felt for him.

Takis sucked in his breath. Nothing about the hotelier's actions where Takis was concerned had been the way he'd thought!

His friends had tried to convince him that the gift of the hotel had been Nassos's way of honoring him for making a success of his life. They'd been right. But without this letter, he'd have gone on threshing around for reasons that had no basis in truth.

He handed it back to her. "Thank you for letting me read it." His voice throbbed. "It's a gift I didn't expect. Because of your generosity I was allowed to see into Nassos's mind. Bless you for that, or I might have gone through the rest of my life being…unsettled."

Those heavenly purple eyes played over his face in confusion. "Why?"

"It's a long story."

"I'd like to hear it. Won't you sit down?"

He couldn't. Takis was too wired. If anyone deserved to know what had been going on inside him, she did. Her honesty and willingness to share something so private humbled him.

"Let me just say I thought Nassos pitied me because of my poor background."

She got to her feet. "I'm sure he did. The grandfather who raised him was ill and so poor, Nassos had to sell the fish he caught from a rowboat so they could live."

Takis's head reared. "I didn't know that."

"I'm not surprised. It pained him to talk about it. My own father's parents died in a ferry accident and a near-destitute aunt took him in, but sadly she too died early. My father and Nassos joined forces and started catching fish to sell so they wouldn't starve."

What she'd just told Takis blew his mind.

"No doubt when he discovered you were working at the hotel and showed such amazing promise after coming from a similar background as himself, he was glad to help you. He was always kind to people.

"If he'd known he was going to die this soon, I have no doubt that he would have given the hotel to you outright. He knew I'd be coming into my inheritance soon and would be able to make my way in the world just fine."

The more she talked, the more ashamed Takis felt for being so far off the mark. These revelations changed everything for him. He cleared his throat. "Do you like running the hotel?"

"Yes, but I haven't known anything else. When I flew to Italy to find you, I thought I might have to track you all the way to New York. My mother's best friend still lives on Long Island. When she came to the funeral, she invited me to stay with her for a while. I've toyed with the idea that if you wanted to work here and be by your family, I'd find a different kind of job in New York."

The thought of her not being here in Crete disturbed him more than a little bit. "You think I need breathing room?"

She cocked her head. "I don't know. *Do* you?"

What Takis needed was to put his priorities in order. His family took precedence over every consideration. Nassos's gift had opened up a way for him to have a legitimate reason to be on Crete for the next six months. But it was vital that as co-owner, she be the visible owner on duty while he was the invisible co-owner who helped behind the scenes.

"I'm going to share something I've never shared

with anyone but my two best friends and business partners. Except for visits to my family, I've been gone from Crete for eleven years. On my last visit here when I attended Nassos's funeral, my mother begged me to come home for good."

"That sounds like a loving mother," Lys said softly. Her genuineness made him believe she was truly happy for him.

"But they've never asked me for anything, or wanted anything from me, whether it be financial or something else. Now I'm worried about them and their health. Maybe I'm wrong about that. Nevertheless I'm planning to sell my hotels in New York and move here permanently to be near them all the time."

"I suspect they've been hoping for that for years."

"If that's true, I'm the last to know." Lys was easy to talk to. She made it comfortable for him, but the warning bells were going off that he was getting in over his head.

"Then you should move here and find out. It would be perfect for you and me. While you run the hotel and live around your parents, I can leave. If I find a new career in New York, then I might not want to buy out your half. In that case, when the six months are up, I'd rather you invested my half of the money from the hotel. Nassos's trust in you is good enough for me."

"I'm flattered that you have more faith in me than I do." But he shook his head, not liking that idea for any reason. Takis didn't want her to leave. It stunned him how strongly attracted he was to her. She was in his blood and he hadn't even kissed her yet. But that day was coming.

"In truth I don't want or need another hotel. The last thing I want is for anyone to know I'm co- owner. Yet for another half year that's the way it has to be and I plan to live out the rest of my life here. So unless your heart is set on going to New York, I'd prefer it if you would call the staff together and tell them you're the new owner of the hotel."

She got to her feet. "But that isn't the truth."

How strange that a few weeks ago he hadn't wanted this gift. Yet in just a short period of time everything had changed. Takis knew himself well and wondered if he could fallen in love with her in such a short space of time. He was overjoyed that for the next six months they'd be forced to remain joined at the hip so to speak.

"No one else needs to know that. I'll explain to Kyrie Pappas why I don't want any mention of me as the co-owner."

Her arched brows knit together. "I don't understand. You're being so mysterious."

"My family must never know my name is tied to the hotel."

She moved closer. "Why?"

"Because I'm a Manolis and there's only room for one Manolis hotel owner on Crete."

A long silence ensued. "You mean your father." She'd read his mind.

"If he knew the kind of gift Nassos had deeded to me—the kind only a father would give to his son—it would hurt him in a way you couldn't comprehend."

"Are you so sure about that?"

"Not entirely, but I love my father."

Tears filled her eyes. "I loved mine too. It's the

only reason I went to Crete with Nassos at the age of seventeen when I didn't want to."

"That had to have been very hard."

"It was in the beginning. I had to leave my friends and school, everything I knew. What I didn't know at the time was that in honoring Baba's wishes, I would learn to love Nassos. He gave me a new life and protected me because he understood a father's love and wanted to honor his best friend's wishes. I get the honor aspect, Takis."

Lys Theron was amazing. "Do you have any idea how grateful I am that you told no one about the will and came all the way to Italy to talk to me in person? Because of you, the secret is still safe."

She studied him for a long time. "I'll keep it. You're worried that if your father knew the truth, he would believe you had a much greater friendship with Nassos than he'd been led to believe. I can see why you think it could ruin your relationship for life."

How did someone so young get to be so wise? "I'm afraid it could," Takis whispered.

"I think you're wrong about it, but no one will ever know from me. I'll talk to Danae so she understands how serious this is to keep absolutely quiet."

No matter his feelings for her, he felt he could trust Lys with his life. "Thank you. But this brings us to our immediate problem. We'll have to conduct business without anyone suspecting the real reason we're together at all."

"What are you suggesting?"

"I've been giving it a lot of thought. When I leave you in a minute, I'm headed straight to the airport. I need to fly back to Milan and talk to my partners.

Among other things I'll have to make preparations to sell my hotel chain in New York and will probably be gone at least a week. When I come back, I'll have a proposition for you."

"Proposition?" she questioned.

"What goes around, comes around," he teased, reminding her of their conversation yesterday when she'd made one to him.

"Aren't you going to give me a hint?" The corner of her sensual mouth lifted, sending a burst of desire through him.

"Not yet. Certain things have to fit into place first."

"You're talking about the hotel in Milan. Do you plan to remain part owner?"

"Possibly." But that wasn't what he had on his mind while she filled his vision to the exclusion of all else. He had plans for them and knew in his gut that she wasn't involved with another man. Otherwise he would have to come up with another idea, but nothing had the appeal of the one he had his heart set on.

"Would you like a ride to the airport? I have an errand to run anyway."

Nothing she'd said could have made him happier. He still wanted to talk to her. "I'd appreciate it."

"I'll just ring Giorgos to let him know my agenda."

"That name isn't familiar to me. What happened to the other manager Nassos relied on in the past?"

"Yannis? He had to retire because his knee operations didn't work out well. He was hard to replace."

"I'm sorry to hear that. Is Giorgos a good manager?"

"Six months ago Nassos hired him as a favor for a close friend, but he had one reservation."

"What was that?"

"He was recently divorced, but he decided to give him a chance."

"Why would that matter?"

"I asked Nassos the same thing. He said it was just a feeling he had that Giorgos might not be able to concentrate on the job, but only time would tell. After the letter Nassos left for me revealing his torment over divorcing Danae, I suppose his concerns about Giorgos made sense. The man moved here from Athens, where he'd been a hotel manager with an excellent reference."

Interesting. "How do you like him so far?"

"I think he's very good at what he does."

"But?"

"I can tell he's lonely."

"Why do you say that?"

"Whenever I start to leave the office, he wants to talk for a while."

Takis struggled not to smile. "Is he attractive?"

"So-so."

"Does he have children?"

"No."

"How old is he?"

"Thirtyish I believe."

A dangerous age. Giorgos must have thought he'd died and arrived in the elysian fields when he discovered Lys on the premises.

While she made the phone call, the proposition he intended to put to her had grown legs.

CHAPTER FIVE

WHEN HER PHONE RANG, Lys had been out on the patio of Danae's villa talking with her about Takis and his fragile relationship with his father. She checked the caller ID before clicking on. "Yes, Giorgos?"

"I don't mean to intrude on your day off, but there was a man at the front desk asking for you a few minutes ago. He didn't leave his name. I told him I'd schedule an appointment, but I needed information first. All he said was that you would know who he was and he'd be back later."

Lys shot to her feet out of breath. *Takis?* But surely he would have phoned her if he'd flown to Crete! He'd been gone a week, but it had felt like a month. Seven days away from him had proven to her how much he had come to mean to her, feelings that went soul deep.

"Did you hear what I said? Do you want security when you return?"

She'd forgotten Giorgos was on the phone. "Was this man threatening in some way?"

"No. But he had an attitude that sounded too familiar and possessive for my liking."

If anyone sounded possessive it was Giorgos, whose observation surprised her. "Thank you for the warning, but I'm not worried. I'll be back at the hotel later."

After hanging up she told Danae what happened. The older woman cocked her head. "Who else could it be but Takis? Aside from Nassos, he's the most exciting man I've *almost* ever bumped into."

Lys chuckled.

"The man's charm is lethal. I have no doubt it rattled Giorgos, who, according to Nassos, was interested in you from the moment he came to work."

"You're kidding—"

This time it was Danae who laughed. "When Nassos realized Giorgos was invisible to you, he stopped worrying that he'd hired him."

"I had no idea I was that transparent."

"There were two or three men you dated that gave us concern because you seemed so swayed by them. We felt you were too young and we ran interference for your sake. But it was when you started seeing Kasmos Loukos, whose father owns the Loukos Shipping lines in Macedonia, we grew very nervous.

"That spoiled young man had already been seen with too many wealthy celebrities. Nassos knew Kasmos was shopping around for the best female prospect to build on his father's fortune. When we saw the way he went about seducing you, we were fearful you might really be in love with him. The problem was, you were an adult. We couldn't do anything about it, and only hoped you could see through him before it was too late."

"Which I did. One night he started talking to me about Nassos, asking questions that were none of his business. That's when a light went on and I remembered all the lessons you'd tried to teach me. I was no longer blinded and told him I didn't want to see him anymore. You should have seen his face—"

"Thank goodness that relationship didn't last! I'm afraid neither Nassos nor I ever thought you'd met your match. Speaking of which, I think you'd better take the helicopter back to the hotel so you can meet up with this mystery man before you die of curiosity."

Heat crept into her cheeks. "I'm not dying," Lys muttered.

"You could have fooled me." She reached for her phone. "I'll alert the pilot."

Lys checked her watch. Ten after one. She'd been here a long time. The two of them were closer than ever. They were family and needed each other while they mourned their loss. No longer did Lys want to go to New York except for a visit to the Farrells'. Her life was here. Takis was here and not going anywhere. *Joy.*

She walked over to hug her. "Have a lovely evening with Stella. Don't get up. I'll see myself out."

"Let me know how this ends."

"You know I will. Love you."

After leaving the villa, she walked out to the pad and climbed on board the helicopter. Within fifteen minutes the pilot landed on top of the Rodino Hotel. She took the elevator to the third floor and freshened up in her suite. With the blood pounding in her ears, she went down to the lobby.

If Takis was here and waiting in the lounge, he'd see her. But since he still hadn't phoned her, she began to think it must have been some other man. Lys couldn't think who that would be unless it was a high-tech salesperson not wanting to go through Giorgos to reach her.

Magda, one of the personnel on duty at the desk, waved her over. "Giorgos told me to watch for you. I'll get him." The woman hurried off before Lys could tell her not to bother.

A second later he came out of his office and walked toward the counter where she was standing. At the same time, she felt two hands slide around her waist from behind.

"Forgive me," Takis whispered. "I have my reason for doing this."

The intimacy brought a small gasp to her lips. She whirled around, meeting those intense hazel eyes that were devouring her.

"Don't look now, but Giorgos is having a meltdown," he murmured. She wouldn't have understood what he meant if she hadn't just had a certain conversation with Danae about the manager. Their mouths were mere centimeters apart. His warm breath on her lips excited her so much, she forgot that she was clinging to his arms. "I'll answer your questions later. Come with me first. We're going for a ride."

Her heart nearly ran away with her as he kept an arm around her shoulders and they left the hotel. Instead of walking her to a taxi, he helped her into a black, middle-of-the-line Acura parked in the registration check-in line. Leon, one of the staff members outside, stared at the two of them in surprise.

Takis started up the engine and darted into the heavy main street traffic in front of the resort. When she could find her voice she said, "This smells brand new."

He flashed her a smile. "I just drove it off the lot. I'm here for the next six months and need transportation." His choice of car made total sense considering the modest income of his family.

"My driving must have frightened you more than I realized."

"Are you saying you would have agreed to be my chauffeur day and night? If so, we'll drive back to the car dealership and turn it in."

Lys laughed gently while he drove them along the harbor road to the Venetian Fortress of Koules. He pulled into a parking space where they could watch the boats.

After shutting off the engine, he turned to her, stretching his arm along the back of the seat. "I owe you an explanation. Thank you for going along with me back there."

"I take it you wanted to make a statement. So why did you do it?"

"In order for us to be together so no one knows the underpinnings of our relationship, I'm proposing we do something shocking. How would you feel about getting engaged to me?"

Engaged?

Lys looked away, literally stunned by what he'd just said.

"Hear me out before you tell me how outrageous I'm being. It could be the one thing that will make it easier to help us achieve our main goal."

"What do you mean?"

"Don't you agree the most important one is for us to get through the next six months honoring Nassos's wishes?"

Her pulse had started to race. "That goes without saying."

"An engagement will give us the perfect cover. While you run the hotel, I'll spend real time with my family. When I whisk you away for a little personal time together, or spend time in your hotel room, no one will know I'm helping you behind the scenes."

Lys struggled to sit still. Nassos had told her Takis was a genius with vision, but this proposition went beyond the boundaries of her imagination. The thought of being engaged to him robbed her of breath.

"The only way the manager will understand why you and I are spending time together and not become suspicious is *if* he thinks we're romantically involved. I was simply setting the scene."

A thrill of alarm passed through her body. "There's no doubt you accomplished your objective a few minutes ago," she said in a tremulous voice.

"It had to be convincing. Tell me something. When you flew to Italy, did the staff know you were leaving the country?"

"Only Giorgos, but I didn't tell him where and let him assume what he wanted."

"That's perfect. Just now it didn't hurt for him and other members of the staff to see us meet in the lobby and assume we have a history away from Crete. When we walked out of the hotel with my arm around you, it no doubt created a new wave of gossip."

"You *know* it did." Being that close to him practically gave her a heart attack.

"If we're engaged, it'll be about you and me for a change. I'm aware the old gossip came close to crucifying you. An engagement would put an end to it."

"I can't imagine anything more wonderful than changing that particular conversation." She took an extra breath. "I'll admit it was awful for Danae too."

He studied her for a moment. "Neither of you deserved this. It pains me for both of you. The new gossip you and I create will cause people to see you in a new light. With a ring on your finger from me, the old news will be forgotten."

She closed her eyes tightly. He was making it sound possible and that increased her nervousness. If this proposal had come from his heart, she'd be in heaven. But it hadn't, and she needed to remember that.

"Lys?" he prodded.

"Can you tell me what you've decided to do about your other businesses?"

"I'm already in negotiations to sell my chain of hotels in New York and invest the money. After talking it over with my partners, I'm going to stay committed to them. The *castello* hotel-restaurant will be the only asset I own and I'll fly to Milan when necessary."

"I'm sure they'll be happy about that." Her voice shook from emotions sweeping through her. "Do your parents know what you've done?"

He nodded. "I've told them I've come home for good and want to help out at the family hotel. My father hasn't said anything about that yet. Lukios has indicated I'm not needed. He explained they would have to let someone else go who must keep their job. I understood that and told him I'd be happy to do some advertising around Crete to bring in more clients."

"What did he say?"

"He shook his head and left the living room with

the excuse that he was needed at the front desk and we'd talk later."

"I'm sorry, but these are early days. Your mother must be ecstatic!"

"I think she's still in shock that I haven't gone back to Italy yet."

"You'll have to give your family time before everyone accepts the fact that you're home permanently. But you have to know she's thrilled, and she's the one to work on. After all, your mother was the one who begged you to come home permanently. In the meantime, you can offer to do little things for her."

Takis studied her intently. "You're a very intuitive woman, so I'm going to take your advice. A few more days and they might be more receptive to the idea of my helping around the hotel. Maybe I'll be able to break my parents down enough so they'll start confiding in me."

Lys moistened her lips nervously. "I'm sure things will get better for you, but I'm afraid you haven't thought out your proposition carefully enough where I'm concerned."

"What do you mean?"

"If you were to tell them we're engaged, it could make things a lot worse for you. I've been in the news recently. Have you thought they might not approve of me?"

His brows furrowed. "If you're the woman I've chosen, they won't say anything no matter their personal feelings. I know that if my mother heard your whole story, she'd be thrilled. Besides, deep down she's had a fear I'd end up with some foreigner and as you're half Cretan, she'll be overjoyed."

"I *am* part foreigner," Lys murmured. "How would you explain our meeting?"

"That's simple. We met at the *castello* hotel in Italy while you were on vacation a while ago. It was love at first sight and we've been together ever since."

His words sank deep in her psyche. It might not have been love at first sight, but a powerful emotion had shaken her to the core when he'd walked in his office to find her there. That emotion continued to grow stronger until she knew he was the man she'd been waiting for all her adult life.

Lys looked away from him. "How will you explain it when we break up in six months and call off the engagement?"

"I don't know. Right now I'm trying to navigate through new waters because of what Nassos has done to us. This situation could have happened forty years from now, but it didn't. You and I are both vulnerable for a variety of reasons and we need to think this through carefully if we're going to do it right."

"I agree."

"Isn't it interesting to realize Nassos had no way of knowing that he'd done me a favor when he deeded me half the hotel. It has forced me to come home and try to make a difference for my family, something I should have done a long time ago."

Lys could feel his pain. "I'm sorry you have the worry of their health on your mind."

"I've been living with it for a while. Maybe I've been wrong and misread what I thought about mother. Just because she has aged a little doesn't mean she's ill."

"That's probably all it is."

"Cesare has accused me of leaping to conclusions. Still, if one of them is ill, I need to find that out. But they're so closed up, it'll take time to pry them open if they're keeping a secret from me. Nothing else is as important to me right now."

"I can relate," her voice trembled. "After Nassos hit his head, he pretended that everything was fine, but I could tell he wasn't himself and it gnawed at me. So I can understand how disturbed you are by your mother's plea that you move back here."

He flicked her an all-encompassing glance. "No matter what, it's my worry. The decision of our getting engaged is up to you. If I see one problem, it's how Danae would feel about it. If neither of you is comfortable with the idea, then we'll figure out another way to proceed."

After Lys's conversation at the villa with Danae earlier in the day, she had no clue how the other woman would react over such an unorthodox idea. But you couldn't compare Takis in the same breath with any other man. Even Danae had admitted as much.

"I—I don't know what Danae will say..." Her voice faltered.

"I realize you love and respect her, and you are uncertain with good reason. Even if Danae could see some value in it, she would probably tell you no. Six months of being engaged to me will prevent you from meeting a man you might want to marry. It will rob you of an important chunk of time out of your life."

"And yours!"

"Let's not worry about that. What matters most to me is to be back with my family where I'm able to make a contribution any way I can and still be a sounding board for you without anyone knowing."

Lys was so confused she couldn't think straight. He'd brought up some valid points that went straight to the heart of their individual dilemmas. But she needed to sort out her thoughts and would have to talk to Danae.

He sat back and turned on the engine. "I need to get home, so I'm going to drive you back to the hotel. I'm in no hurry for a decision. There's no deadline. I'll leave it up to you to contact me when you want to discuss hotel business."

Before long he pulled up in front of the hotel. Lys could tell he was anxious to leave. "We'll talk soon, Takis. Take care."

"Just a minute." He leaned across and kissed her briefly on the mouth. She couldn't believe what had just happened. "I needed that," he whispered before she opened the door and got out.

Her heart thudding, she rushed past Leon without acknowledging him. Her only desire was to get to her room where she could react to his kiss in private. After what he'd just done, the thought of a fake engagement to Takis had caused her heart to pound to a feverish pitch. She feared she was already running a temperature. When she could gather her wits, Lys would phone Danae. They needed to talk.

Takis drove to Tylissos, still savoring the taste of Lys, whose succulent mouth was a revelation. He'd never be the same again.

Before long he stopped by the children's hospital. After phoning his mother to find out if she needed him to do any errands for her, he discovered that Kori had taken Cassia to the doctor because of another asthma attack. It meant she'd been forced to leave her part-time work at the restaurant. Takis told his mother he'd look in on them.

He found his older sister holding his niece in her arms while she recovered after the medication they'd given her.

"Tak-Tak," his little niece cried when she saw him enter the room and held out her arms. Takis gathered her to him and gave her a gentle hug, kissing her neck.

"Do you feel better now?"

"*Nay*. Go home."

Takis looked at his sister, who had the same dark auburn hair as her daughter, the color of cassia cinnamon. "Did the doctor say she could leave?"

"Yes, but I have to wait until Deimos goes off shift to pick us up."

"But that won't be until nine thirty tonight. Tell you what. I'm going to slip out and buy an infant seat for my car. Then I'll drive you to work."

"You have a car?"

"I bought one this morning. I need transportation now that I'm back for good."

She stared hard at him. "You're really going to live here again?"

He nodded. "I never planned to be gone this long. Now that I'm home, I'm staying put." Just being here to help his sister let him know he'd done the right thing to come back to Greece for good.

Takis handed a protesting Cassia to her mother. "This won't take me long. When I get back, I'll run you by the restaurant and take her to the hotel with me." His mother tended Cassia when Kori had to go to work.

Her face looked tired but her light gray eyes lit up. "Are you sure?"

"There's nothing I'd love more." He leaned over to give them both a kiss on the cheek. "See you in a few minutes."

Takis hurried out of the hospital and drove to a local store, where he bought a rear-facing and two forward-facing car seats. That way he could take all his nieces and nephews to the park at once.

Within a half hour he was back and had fastened Cassia in her new seat. He would put in the other seats when he had the time. Kori sat next to him while he drove her to the Vrakas restaurant, where Deimos cooked traditional Cretan cuisine.

"Don't worry about anything. I'll take good care of her."

"I know that. She loves you. So do I." Her eyes filled with tears. "Thank you. I'm so glad you've come home." Her love meant everything to Takis.

After she hurried inside, he chatted with Cassia during the short ride to the old Manolis Hotel. He pulled around the back next to his father's truck. Lukios's car wasn't here, which meant he'd gone to his house a block away. Both his brother and sister lived nearby.

"Come on, sweetheart." He lifted her out of the seat and entered the private back door where his parents had lived in their own apartment since their marriage. "Mama? Look who I've got with me!" His mother came running from the kitchen into the living room. "She's breathing just fine now."

"Ah!" She pulled Cassia into her arms. "Come with me and I'll give you some grape juice." Grapes grew in profusion on this part of Crete.

"Tak-Tak!" his niece called to him, not wanting to be parted from him. He smiled because she couldn't say the *is* part yet. He grinned at his mother, who laughed.

"I'm right behind you, Cassia."

While his father was busy with hotel business, he had his mother to himself in the kitchen. She put a plate of his favorite homemade *dakos* on the table, a combination of rusk, feta cheese, olives and tomatoes. Cassia sat in the high chair drinking her juice while he devoured six of them without taking a breath and finished off the moussaka.

Afterward he held Cassia and read to her from a bundle of children's books he'd brought her on his last trip home. She had a favorite called *Am I Small?* He had to read it to her over and over again.

The little Greek girl in the story asked every animal she met if she was small. It had a surprise ending. Cassia couldn't wait for it. Neither could Takis, who was totally entertained by her responses.

At quarter to ten, Kori ran into the apartment and found her daughter asleep in his arms. She thanked him with a hug and hurried out to the car where Deimos was waiting for them.

Takis turned out lights and went to bed in the guest room he used whenever he came home for a visit. However, now that he was back for good, he needed to figure out where to live. Tomorrow he'd look around the neighborhood and find a house like his brother's and Kori's, close to the hotel.

Takis took a long time to get to sleep, knowing the nub of his restlessness had to do with a certain female who'd come to live in his heart. They weren't engaged yet, but the way he was feeling, he didn't know how he was going to keep his desire for her to himself much longer. Earlier in the car he'd kissed her, but it hadn't lasted long enough and he'd been forced to restrain himself.

The next morning, he installed the other two car seats before visiting a Realtor in the village. By late afternoon he'd finally been shown a small Cretan stone house he liked with a beautiful flowering almond tree. It had been up for sale close to a year and was two blocks away from the hotel. The place suited him with two bedrooms upstairs and a little terrace over the lower main rooms covered in vines.

Takis stood in the kitchen while they talked about the need to paint the interior and upgrade the plumbing. The house would do for him and not stand out. While he and the Realtor finished up the negotiations, his cell phone rang. One check of the caller ID caused his adrenaline to kick in. He swiped to accept the call.

"Lys?"

"I'm glad you answered." She sounded a little out of breath. "Can you talk?"

"In a few minutes I'll be free for the rest of the evening."

"I just flew back from Kasos." She'd been with Danae. "How soon can you meet me at my suite?" The fact that she wanted to see him right away might not be good news, but he refused to think that way.

"I have a better idea. I'll pick you up in front of

the hotel in a half hour. There's something I want to show you. We'll talk then."

"All right. I'll be ready."

He hung up and thanked the Realtor, who drove them back to his office. The older man handed him the keys to the house. Takis walked outside to his car with a sense of satisfaction that he was now a home-owner on Crete, the land of his ancestors.

En route to Heraklion, he stopped for some takeout of his favorite foods; rosemary-flavored fried snails, *Sfaki* pies and a Greek raki liqueur made from grapes. He liked the idea of sharing his first meal in his own home with Lys where they could be alone.

Before long he reached the hotel. Lys stood out from everyone when he pulled up in front. Her black blouse and dark gray skirt made the perfect foil for the tawny gold hair he was dying to run his hands through. He leaned across and opened the door for her.

"Hi!" Lys climbed in the front, bringing her flowery fragrance with her. "Umm. Something smells good," she remarked as he drove away and headed out of town.

"I'm hungry and thought we could eat after we reach our destination."

"Where are we going?"

"To Tylissos. I bought a house today and thought you might like to see it."

She made a strange sound in her throat. "Already?"

"My parents' apartment is small. They don't need another person underfoot while they tend my niece during the day. She naps on the bed I use while I'm here."

"How old is she?"

"Cassia is three. I'm crazy about her. The cute little thing has chronic asthma. Yesterday my sister had to take her to the hospital so the doctor could help her, but she's back home now."

"Oh, the poor darling."

"She handles it like there's nothing wrong. Now tell me about you. I take it you've had a talk with Danae."

"Yes."

The short one-syllable answer could mean anything. "Is it a good or bad sign that you can't look at me? Don't you know I'm fine with whatever you have to say?" At least that's what he was telling himself right this minute.

"After discussing everything with Danae, she surprised me so much I'm not sure what I am supposed to say."

He left that answer alone and drove into Tylissos and it wasn't long before he pulled up next to a house on the corner. "We've arrived."

While she got out, he reached for the bag of food on the backseat. After they walked to the front door, he put the key in the lock and opened it. "Welcome to my humble abode. I'm afraid we'll have to eat in the kitchen standing up."

Her chuckle reminded him not everyone had such a pleasant nature. So far there wasn't anything about her he didn't love. While she wandered around, he put their cartons of food on the counter next to the utensils.

After a minute, she came back and they started to eat. "Your house is charming, especially the terrace."

"Best seen at twilight." The house needed work from the main floor up.

"Takis—"

They both smiled in understanding. It felt right to be here with her like this. He'd never known such a moment of contentment and wanted to freeze it.

Once he'd poured the *raki* into plastic cups, he handed one to her. *"To our health,"* he said in Greek. They drank some before he asked her what Danae had said. She kept drinking. "Why are you so reticent to tell me?"

Her frown spoke volumes. "I wish I hadn't talked to her at all."

"Why?"

"Because she thinks an engagement could be a good idea for the reasons you suggested, but she says it doesn't go far enough."

"What does she mean?"

"Her blessing is contingent on us taking the engagement a step further, which makes this whole discussion ridiculous."

"How much further?"

She shook her head. "None of it matters."

"It does to me. Go on."

"I told Danae about everything you confided in me concerning your relationship with your family, especially your father. She was very sympathetic, but she's convinced they won't believe you're serious about living here for good unless we put a formal announcement of our engagement in the paper."

Elated with that response, he said, "I tend to agree with her."

Lys looked surprised. "That's not all," she murmured, not meeting his eyes.

"What's wrong?"

"She says we'll have to put a wedding date in the announcement, but the paper won't publish it if the date is longer than three months away. That's so soon!"

A strange sensation shot through Takis. If he believed in such things, he had the feeling Nassos had spoken through Danae. No one could sew up a deal like Nassos, covering all the bases. "What reason did she give?"

"I was raised in the Greek Orthodox church and so were you. She knows your parents are traditionalists. Because of the scandal that surrounded me after Nassos died, a promise of marriage to me in the writeup will show their friends and neighbors that you never believed the gossip about me.

"Danae said that in honoring me that way, they'll see you intend to be a good, loyal husband and they'll be happy you've come home for good. Every parent wants to see his or her child making plans to settle down and have a family. Anything less than a newspaper announcement with a wedding date won't carry the necessary weight."

The woman was brilliant. "Danae's right. Did she say anything else?"

After pacing the floor, she came to a halt. "Yes. After knowing your history, she says she likes you and approves of you for my husband. She knows Nassos would approve of you too."

That sounded exactly like something Nassos would have said in order to protect Lys. "I'm humbled by her opinion. She's a true Cretan. The more I think about it, the more I know she's right about everything she said. How do you feel about it?" The blood hammered in his ears while he waited for her answer.

"I—I didn't expect her to be so direct," she stammered.

"You still haven't answered my question. Does it upset you that I'm the first man Danae has ever approved of for you?"

Her knuckles turned white while her hands clenched the edge of the counter. "I'm not upset."

"Then why are you so tense?"

"We're not in love! We don't intend to actually get married—" Lys protested. "It would hurt your family too much to pretend something that won't happen. I told Danae as much, so we'll forget the whole idea of an engagement."

His eyes narrowed on her features. "I don't want to forget any of it. The idea of marrying you appeals to me more and more."

A quiet gasp escaped her lips. "Please be serious, Takis."

"I've never been more serious in my life. When I first suggested the idea of getting engaged, my main concern was to fit in with my family again and it seemed the perfect way to do it. But now I find that I want to be married, and Danae is right. Three months will be a perfect amount of time to grow close before we get married."

Color filled her cheeks. "We'd probably end up not being able to stand each other!"

Someone was on his side. Lys hadn't said no to the whole idea because she loved Danae and listened to her. "That's the whole point of an engagement, isn't it? To find out how we really feel? I know how I really feel at this moment."

In the next breath, he pulled her into his arms. After kissing her long and hard, he relinquished her mouth. "Do you think you could see yourself living in this house as my wife? I'd give you free reign to furnish it any way you like."

"Don't say any more," she cried softly and eased away from him. "You told me you want acceptance from your family. I can promise you that won't happen when they find out I'm the daughter of the man who gave you your first job in New York. I represent everything that took you away from them in the first place."

When he'd confided in her at his lowest ebb, she'd taken his pain to heart. Unfortunately, he'd done too good a job and needed to turn this around.

"Besides the fact that I left Crete of my own free will, keep in mind we didn't meet until a few weeks ago. When I tell them I've found the woman I want to marry, you have nothing to worry about."

CHAPTER SIX

THE WOMAN HE wanted to marry?

After the intensity of that kiss, Lys was dying to believe him. Deep in her heart she wanted marriage to Takis with every atom in her body, but she was too confused to think.

Astounded by the strength of her feelings, she said, "It's getting dark… I need to get back to the hotel."

Ignoring him, she put everything in the bag except the bottle of liqueur, which she left on the counter. They walked out of the house and Lys hurried to his car. As she put the bag in the backseat, Takis caught up with her and slid behind the wheel.

"On the way home I'll drive you past the Manolis Hotel. It looks like something Cassia would build with her blocks. Two for the bottom floor and one for the top."

Several turns brought them to the main street where the buildings sprang from the cement and had grown side by side. Because of his description, she picked it out immediately, painted in yellow with dark-brown-framed windows and matching tiles on the roof. A sign hung over the bottom right entrance.

He stopped in front, not pressing her to talk about

anything. During the last eleven years, she assumed nothing here had changed in all that time. She thought about the eighteen-year-old boy who'd wanted to help expand his father's hotel business. Instead, he'd ended up in New York thanks to Nassos and her father. Now he'd come full circle and was back for good.

"What are you thinking?"

She took a deep breath. "That you've accomplished miracles in your life."

His features took on a grim cast. "I'll take the one that hasn't happened yet."

She presumed he was talking about his relationship with his father. Her heart ached for what he was going through.

He started driving again and they headed for Heraklion. "Since you know where I'll be living and how I'm spending my time, I'll leave it up to you to decide when you want to get together to talk business."

Nassos couldn't have known his will would put them in such a difficult position. In Italy Takis had told Cesare he didn't want the hotel, let alone the complication of it being tied to Lys.

"Takis? Are you worried that if we don't get engaged, somehow word will reach your father that there's another reason you're tied to the hotel when we're seen together?"

"Anything's possible, but I'll deal with it by Skyping with you on the computer when you feel the need for a meeting."

"I still wouldn't do that in the office where Giorgos or one of the staff could walk in."

"Then we'll do it from your hotel room."

By the time he'd driven up in front of the hotel,

she was in torment. He got out and came around to open her door. "I'll be working on my house for the next week. If anything comes up, give me a call. *Kalinikta,* Lys."

"Good night," she whispered. "Thank you for the delicious food."

"You're welcome," he whispered against her lips before kissing her. Lys's attraction to him was overpowering. Obeying a blind need, she kissed him back again and again, relishing the slight rasp that sent tingles of desire through her body. After that, she found the strength to dash inside the hotel entrance to the elevators.

With pounding heart she reached her room, filled with unassuaged longings. After a minute when she had caught her breath, she called the front desk to find out if there were any messages for her. Thankful when she learned there was nothing pressing, she hung up and took a shower.

Lys had hoped to fall asleep watching TV, but she couldn't concentrate. Throughout the night she tossed and turned. Her fear that Takis's father would learn about Nassos's willed gift wouldn't leave her alone. Her mind relived what Danae had told her, that she approved of Takis and felt he'd make the right husband for her. Lys was so in love, she wanted him for her husband.

Takis hadn't asked for Nassos's gift. Who would have dreamed he would pass away this early in life? Nassos hadn't known the degree of fragility between Takis and his father, otherwise he wouldn't have put Takis in this situation. Nassos would have found another way to show his admiration.

When morning came, she felt like she hadn't slept at all and knew she had to see Takis again. He'd become her whole life! After eating breakfast in her room, she dressed in dark brown pleated pants with a matching-colored long-sleeved sweater.

Once she'd run a brush through her hair and had applied an apricot frost lipstick, she went down to the office to return phone calls and talk to some vendors. She texted Danae that she'd call her later in the day. Lys wasn't prepared to talk to her yet.

Around noon she told Giorgos she was leaving without giving him a reason and headed for the parking garage before he could detain her. Giorgos couldn't hide his frustration that she'd been avoiding him. Takis had planted a seed. Clearly it had taken root.

Once out on the road, she made several stops to buy souvlaki, fruit and soda. All the way to Takis's house she hoped she'd see his car parked outside. To her relief she did find the car there and parked behind it. Anxious to talk to him, she grabbed the sack of food and hurried to the front door. After knocking twice with no response, she tried the handle. To her surprise it opened.

"Takis?" she called out. "Are you here?" No answer. She crossed through to the kitchen and saw a couple of old wooden chairs and a card table. On the counter he'd left a coffee thermos. He must have gone somewhere. Maybe he'd gotten hungry and had walked to the hotel that was only a few blocks away.

She put the food on the table knowing he'd be back or he wouldn't have left the door unlocked. While she waited for him, she went up the small staircase to the second floor. Both tiny bedrooms were separated by a bathroom that needed work. And before she could prevent the thought from forming, she decided that one of the bedrooms would make a perfect nursery.

Each had a door that opened onto the terrace. You would need a railing if you brought children over here. In her mind's eye she could picture a lovely table with a colorful umbrella surrounded by chairs and pots of flowers.

Beyond the village the view looked out on the ancient Minoan site with its archaeological ruins, reminding her of the statue of King Minos on Takis's desk in Italy.

While she stood there near the edge, deep in thought, she saw a pickup truck turn the corner and pull up behind her car. All kinds of equipment filled the bed. Her pulse raced as she saw two men get out. The taller of the two, an Adonis dressed in jeans and a white T-shirt, looked up and waved to her.

"*Yassou*, Lys! I'll be in as soon as I unload the truck!"

"Let me help!"

Excited he'd come, she hurried downstairs and opened the front door. His brother—it couldn't be anyone else with those features—had red tinges in his dark blond hair. He brought in a ladder and some paint cans. Takis followed, carrying other paint equipment and drop cloths.

His eyes, that marvelous hazel green, played over her. "I'm glad you're here." His deep velvety voice wound its way through her body, igniting her senses. He put everything down in the living room. "Lukios?

I'd like you to meet Lys Theron. Lys? This is Lukios Manolis."

Takis had told her that Lukios hadn't been friendly the other day. Lys had hoped for his sake that his brother would warm up. It appeared they were getting along better now and that knowledge made her happy.

"You're the wonderful brother he's told me about. It's so nice to meet you. I've been anxious to meet Takis's family." She smiled and put out her hand.

The other man shook it. "How do you do," he said in a subdued voice. His eyes swerved back and forth at the two of them, trying to figure things out. She had no doubt he'd seen her in the news.

"I thought Takis might be hungry while he worked, so I brought lunch. It's in the kitchen. He has such a big appetite, I bought enough for half a dozen people. Please feel welcome to eat with us if you'd like."

He looked taken back. "Thank you. Have you known each other long?"

Without giving Takis a chance to answer, she said, "Quite a while. We met in Italy while I was on vacation. Those were your children in the photos I saw on his desk at work? Both yours and your sister, Kori's. They are adorable. Your parents must be crazy about their grandchildren."

"They are," he murmured.

"In case you didn't know yet, Takis asked me to marry him yesterday and brought me here to see where we're going to live."

Lukios blinked. "I had no idea."

"He surprised me too." She smiled at him. "Since he told me I could decorate it any way I want, I decided to start with a housewarming present by offering my services to help with the painting."

"How come *I'm* so lucky?" Takis interjected, as if they had no audience. His eyes gleamed.

She knew what her response had meant to him and heat swept through her body. By throwing herself into his suggestion for an engagement, she had no choice but to be a hundred percent committed and go all the way.

"This is such a cozy house, I'm anxious to see how we can bring it to life."

Takis moved closer. "All I brought with me today is the primer for the walls. After we've put it on, we'll go to the paint store and decide on the best color for the rooms."

Lys had really done it now! She'd taken him by complete surprise, but it hadn't thrown him. Nothing did. Takis was always several steps ahead no matter the situation. His responses since coming in the house had to have convinced his brother that their relationship was all but sealed.

"Come in the kitchen, Lukios. Let me serve you while you tell me about your family. What is your wife's name? I'm sure Takis told me, but I can't remember."

"It's Doris."

"That's it. I had a friend in school named Doris too! I understand your two children are older than Cassia."

He blinked, as if he were surprised she knew so much. "Paulos and Ava. They're four and five."

"What a blessing. I always wanted siblings, but

my mother died when I was little. My father never remarried, so it was just me."

"That must have been hard."

"Yes, but I had a father I adored."

While she served him on a paper plate, Takis helped himself and stayed in the background of the conversation. She took it that he didn't mind that she'd more or less taken over and was chatting away.

"Is Doris a stay-at-home mother?"

"No. She works with me at the hotel."

"How terrific for both of you." She handed him some tangerines.

He peeled one and ate the whole thing at once, reminding her of Takis's eating habits. "You think that's a good idea?"

Ah. He was coming to life. "If I loved my husband, I'd want to be with him as much as possible. She's a lucky woman." Poor Danae would have loved to work with Nassos like that…

Lukios darted Takis a glance, but she pretended not to notice. "Do you want a Pepsi? It's the only soda I could find."

"Thank you."

She turned to Takis. "What about you?"

"I'll drink one later. Why don't you sit and I'll wait on you?"

Their gazes met. "I'd love it."

After she finished eating, Lukios got up from his chair and put his empty plate on the table. "Thank you for the lunch. It was very nice to meet you, Kyria Theron."

"I'm thrilled I got to be introduced to you at last."

"It was my pleasure. Now I'm afraid I have to get *Baba*'s truck back to the hotel. Work is waiting."

Takis put down his soda. "I'll see you out, Lukios." He leaned over and kissed her cheek. "Don't go away," he whispered. "I'll be right back."

He walked out of the kitchen, leaving her trembling. She was a fool to be this happy when it wasn't a real engagement, but she couldn't help it. There was no one like Takis.

A few minutes later Takis came back in the kitchen and found Lys cleaning up. "You're a sight I never expected to see in here after leaving you in front of the hotel last evening."

She looked up at him. "I'm sure you didn't. But I couldn't sleep during the night because of worry over your secret getting out. I remembered back to that day in your office in Italy. When you saw the deed, the shock on your face stunned me."

He stared at her. *It wasn't just the deed, Lys Theron.*

"Later, after your return to Heraklion, we talked about what Nassos had done by giving you co-ownership of the hotel. That's when I realized why you worried it could be damaging to your relationship with your father if he knew."

"I shouldn't have said anything to you about that."

"I'm glad you did. I—I want you to be able to preserve that precious bond with your father," she stammered from emotion. "I loved mine so much."

He leaned against the doorjamb with his strong arms folded. "So you've decided to be the sacrificial lamb."

"I don't think of my decision that way and hope you don't either."

"Be honest. You'd do anything for Nassos and Danae."

She threw her head back. "I guess I would."

And now she was willing to help preserve his father's love by entering into an engagement of convenience. If Lys knew the depth of Takis's feelings for her, would she admit she couldn't live without him either and toss the pretense away? He cocked his head. "You realize my brother swallowed your act so completely, he gave me a hug for luck before getting in the truck."

Luck? Her heart leaped. "He isn't the hugging type?" she teased.

"After what I told you about him, you know he isn't. The last time it happened, my girlfriend had just died."

"Oh, Takis—how awful that must have been. Is it still too hard to talk about?"

"No. I remember there was pain, but I don't feel it anymore."

"What happened to her?"

"I was working at the hotel in Heraklion the day Gaia took a bus trip with her friends. It was the high school's year-end retreat. They went to the Samaria Gorge."

"I've heard of it but have never been there," Lys murmured.

"It's a place in the White Mountains where it's possible to hike down along the gorge floor past streams, wild goats, deserted settlements and steep cliffs. The plan was for them to reach the village of Agia Roumeli and take a boat back to the bus for the return trip to Tylissos.

"The tragedy occurred when a tourist drifted across the road and hit the bus, causing it to roll over and down the side of the gorge. There were thirty students on the bus. Three of them died. One of them was Gaia."

She buried her face in her hands. "I'm so sorry."

"Her death prompted me to accept Nassos's offer to leave for the States and go to work for the man whom I now know was your father. After her funeral, the move to New York helped me get over it."

Lys nodded and wiped her eyes. "Had you been close for a long time?"

"From the age of fifteen."

"How terrible." She shook her head. "Does her family still live here?"

"Yes."

"Do you visit them?"

"Only once, the first time I came back to be with my parents. They didn't need to see me as a reminder. One look at the framed picture of her on the end table was enough to prevent me from dropping in on them again."

"What about the latest woman in your life now? Will news of your engagement hurt her?"

He strolled toward her. "I've had several short-lived relationships, none of them earthshaking, as the Americans have a way of saying. For the last three years I've been consumed with earning a living and haven't allowed any serious entanglements to get in the way."

Her purple gaze fused with his. "And there you

were, minding your own business at the *castello* when destiny dropped in to change your life yet again."

Obeying a strong impulse, he put his hands on her shoulders. Takis could feel her heartbeat through her soft cashmere sweater.

"I watched you walk out of the church at the funeral and thought you were the most beautiful woman I'd ever seen in my life. If I hadn't had to catch a plane for Athens right then, I would have gone to the cemetery in order to meet you and learn your name."

"I had no idea," she murmured.

"You'll never know my wonder when I entered my office and discovered the daughter of Kristos Theron standing in front of Nassos's photograph with tears in her eyes. That was my first shock, followed by another one in the form of the deed that bound you and me together in an almost mystical way. Today I received a third shock to find you here waiting for me."

"I shouldn't have come in, but you left the door unlocked. I hope you didn't mind."

"Mind?" His hands slid to her upper arms and squeezed them. "To convince Lukios is half the battle. You did something for me in front of my brother I couldn't have done for myself. After my years abroad, he's in shock I've found my soul mate in Crete, when he didn't think it was possible."

Takis hadn't thought it could ever happen either.

"Had you mentioned me to him before today?"

"Never."

"What about your sister?"

"She's always on my side. Just so you know, when I walked him out to the truck, he brought up nothing about you. If he recognized you from the newspaper, he didn't mention it. That should tell you a lot."

Her eyes glistened with moisture. "Then I'm glad."

"Glad enough to come with me and get your engagement ring? When I introduce you to my parents, I want it on your finger."

He could see her throat working. "I thought you were going to paint today."

"I'm getting things ready, but will have to wait until tomorrow morning. The water and electricity won't be turned on until then. Since we've eaten, let's drive into Heraklion."

Without her saying anything, she walked with him to his car. After they headed for the city she turned to him. "You mustn't buy me anything that stands out."

"I've already bought it."

A slight gasp escaped her throat.

He smiled. "The ring *does* have unique significance, but don't worry. It's not a ten-carat blue-white diamond from Tiffany's worth three million dollars."

"When did you get it?"

"The day I suggested the engagement. Once I visualize an idea, I act on it. I'm afraid it's the way I'm made."

"You're one amazing man."

"Amazing as in crazy, insane, exasperating? What?"

"All three and more."

He chuckled. "I don't want to hear the rest. Admit you like me a little."

She looked away.

"Why don't you pull out your phone and we'll compose an engagement announcement for the newspaper. The sooner it gets in, the better."

"Danae will want to check it over first." She pressed the note app. He watched her get started. "I think it should begin with something like Kyria Danae Rodino is pleased to announce the engagement of Lys Theron to Takis Manolis, son of Nikanor and—" She paused and turned to him. "What's your mother's name?"

"Hestia."

"Goddess of the hearth. What a lovely name." She typed it in and finished with, "Son of Nikanor and Hestia Manolis of Tylissos, Crete."

His hands gripped the steering wheel a little tighter. "You need to add Lys Theron, daughter of Kristos and Anna Theron."

A small cry escaped. "I didn't know you knew my mother's name."

"Someone at the hotel told me after I started working there. As for the rest of the announcement, we can figure out the June date after you talk to Danae. Then end it with saying that the wedding will take place in the Greek Orthodox church in Heraklion."

"Which one were your parents married in?"

"Agios Titos. That's where we'll take our vows."

He was living for it.

CHAPTER SEVEN

TAKIS DROVE TO a specialty shop called Basil. It was located next to the Archaeological Museum of Heraklion that sold Minoan replicas the tourists could afford. He parked the car and walked her inside.

"I love this place! When I first came to Crete, Danae brought me in here every time we took visiting friends of theirs through the museum. We'd always buy a few trinkets."

He guided her past clusters of people to the counter where he asked one of the clerks to get the owner. "Basil is holding a ring for me." Takis couldn't wait to slide it on her finger. He wanted her in his arms and his life forever.

"A moment, please."

"Look at this, Takis!" Lys walked over to a fresco hanging on the wall representing a Minoan prince. He stood in his horse-drawn chariot holding the reins. A warrior on the road handed him a drink from a golden cup. "I've seen this in the museum. It's a splendid replica. Can't you see it hanging over your fireplace?"

"Don't you mean ours?"

"Yes. This is all still new to me."

He hugged her around the waist. Her interest intrigued him. "Why do you like it so much?"

"The plain with those trees where he's riding reminds me of the view from your terrace. Danae once took me out to the Tylissos archaeological site not far from your village. You have Cretan blood in your veins and live in a Cretan historical spot that's over seven thousand years old."

He smiled. "You were born in New York, which dates back ten thousand years."

"Except that I'm half-Cretan and I don't have part Native American blood. My mother was American through and through. Somehow it doesn't seem the same."

A chuckle escaped his lips, enjoying their conversation more than she would ever know. *"Touché."* He gave her a brief kiss on the mouth, unable to resist tasting her whenever he could.

"Kyrie Manolis!" He turned around to see the owner come up to him.

"*Kalispera*, Basil."

The older man stared in wonder at Lys like most men did, unable to help it. "You've brought your beautiful fiancée. Now I understand your choice of stone. Come with me."

Takis guided her over to another counter. Basil went around behind. On the glass he set a small gold box with a *B* on it and took off the lid. Takis heard her sharp intake of breath when the owner handed the ring to Lys.

"This is incredible." Her voice shook.

Takis had hoped for that reaction.

"It's a replica of old Minoan jewelry," Basil explained.

"I know. I've seen one like it in the museum."

"Look closely. The three-quarter-inch band is intricately linked by twelve layers of tiny gold ropes, some braided, some mesh. The middle one represents the snake of the snake goddess, known for being gracious, sophisticated and intelligent.

"This ring would be identical to the one you saw in the museum, but your fiancé wanted a cut glass purple stone instead of the red garnet in the center. Put it on and we'll see if it fits."

After she slid it on to her ring finger, her eyes flew to Takis. He'd never seen them glow before. "This is too much. Thank you." She kissed him on the side of his jaw.

Basil laughed. "If the ring was authentic, he would be paying over five million euros at auction. But the beauty of shopping with Basil is that it didn't cost that much."

"It looks like the real thing."

"My artisans are highly qualified. Does it mean you are pleased?"

"How could I not be?" she told him.

Takis kissed her, uncaring that they had an audience. Color suffused her cheeks.

"Wear it in joy, *despinis.*"

Takis pocketed the box. "Before we leave, I'll buy the fresco on the wall over there." He pulled out some bills and left them on the counter.

"Put your money away. I have more of those in the back room. This will be my early wedding present for you. You two are so much in love, I think you must get married soon. One of my clerks will wrap it."

After Basil walked away, Lys looked up at Takis. "Will your family believe you didn't spend a lot of money on this?"

"They'll *know* I didn't when I tell Kori it came from Basil's. She shops here every so often because it isn't expensive. If anything, she'll tell me a snake ring isn't at all romantic. She'll pity you for getting engaged to a man whose mind is steeped in Cretan history."

"Then she'll be surprised when I tell her my Cretan father immersed me in the culture too."

As Takis marveled over his feelings for her, Basil hurried over to them with the wrapped fresco. "Here you are."

Takis thanked him and they all shook hands. Then he walked her out to the parking lot and put it in the backseat.

"I think we need to celebrate our engagement. Where would you like to go before we drive back to the house?"

"I need to phone Danae before we do anything else. Do you mind?"

"Why would I? We're not in any hurry."

He listened while she made the call. After a short conversation, she hung up. "She'd like us to fly to the villa for dinner. How do you feel about that?"

"It's perfect. We can go over the final draft of our announcement with her."

"She'll alert the pilot that we're on our way."

"Good." Full of adrenaline, he drove them to the hotel.

"You can park in my spot. I'll show you."

Leon had seen them together enough to wave him on through. Takis helped her out of the car and locked it. After putting his arm around her shoulders, they walked to the bank of elevators. The feel of her body brushing against his side lit him on fire.

When they passed Giorgos in the main hallway, the other man said, "Lys—you've a dozen messages on your desk."

"Any emergencies?"

"No."

"Then I'll get to them later. Thanks."

Before long they climbed in the helicopter and headed for the island. Lys kept examining the ring. All of a sudden she flashed him a glance. "You were right when you said this would have unique significance."

His brows lifted. "You think Danae will approve?"

"She'll probably tell you she can see why Nassos found you such an amazing young man."

Within a half hour they'd arrived at the fabulous villa, a place that reflected the personality of the famous hotelier. Danae had a feast prepared with some of Lys's favorite fish dishes. As they walked through to the dining room the housekeeper was pouring them snifters of Metaxa, a smooth Greek brandy Takis loved.

Danae stood at the head of the table. "Before we eat, I'd like to make a toast to the two of you. May this engagement smooth the path with your family and take away some of the sadness in Lys's heart."

Amen.

"Wait! I have a surprise." She went over to the

sideboard and brought Lys a gift wrapped in plain paper.

"What's this?"

"I found it in the bottom drawer of Nassos's dresser while I was cleaning out the penthouse. When I opened it, I remembered. After Kristos's funeral, Nassos brought this back to give you one day for a special occasion. It was a small painting of Kasos Island that he once gave your mom." Danae smiled at Lys. "I think this is the perfect occasion now that you're wearing Takis's ring."

Takis could tell Lys's hands were trembling as she undid the paper. "Oh, Danae." Tears spilled down her cheeks. "This is so wonderful. I'll always cherish it."

Danae had just given Takis another reason to like the woman Nassos had married.

Lys quickly wrapped it up and put it on the empty chair next to her. "Thank you, Danae."

"Consider that it came from Nassos, who was born here too."

"I'm so touched he kept it all this time."

"He loved you." Her gaze flicked to Takis, after glancing at Lys's hand. "In my opinion you couldn't have chosen a more perfect ring for Lys, who was fascinated with Minoan culture from the time she first came to live with us."

"I could tell that," Takis said after taking another drink of brandy. "She was so taken with one of the frescoes at Basil's, I bought it for her."

Danae's glance fell on Lys. "I bet it was the prince in the chariot."

"Danae—"

The older woman kept right on talking. "Lys

wasn't so different from little girls everywhere, but she was never one to buy posters of the latest rock stars to hang on her bedroom wall. A Cretan warrior was her idea of perfection."

Two hours later they flew back to the hotel. To her relief, Danae hadn't expounded anymore on the fresco. She could have told Takis that Lys had taken one look at the prince years ago when they'd seen the real fresco in the museum, and had fallen in love on sight. The fact that he bore a strong resemblance to Takis was something she knew Danae would tease her about quite mercilessly the next time they were alone.

Only now did Lys remember Takis saying he'd tell his parents it was love at first sight after meeting her. But there was one difference.

Lys *had* fallen in love with him. For real.

She knew it to the very core of her being. From here on out she had to be careful he didn't find out how she really felt about him.

This engagement was on slippery ground because he was acting like a man in love who wanted to marry her. During dinner he'd shown excitement over the June 4 wedding date Danae had suggested. Lys would be the greatest fool alive if she started to believe that she might be able to have what she desired most in the secret recess of her heart.

At ten thirty they got out of the helicopter and headed for the elevator. Takis held the door so it wouldn't close. "Why don't I come by for you in the morning? We'll stop to eat somewhere on the way to my house. Your car will be safe parked outside tonight."

"I'm not worried about that." He noticed her clutching the gift in her arm. "What time were you thinking?"

"Since you're running the hotel, you need to take care of those phone calls Giorgos told you about. So why don't you call me when you're ready and I'll come for you."

"All right."

He allowed the doors to close and they rode to the third floor, where he walked her to her room. Lys was so afraid that he might want to come in and she would let him, she was totally thrown when he told her he needed to get going. After giving her a quick kiss on the cheek, he turned away and strode down the hall to the elevator.

She felt totally bereft. *You idiot, Lys!*

After entering her suite, she put the gift on the coffee table and left to go downstairs. Lys was too wound up to go to bed yet. When she entered the office she found Giorgos still at the front desk talking with Chloe, who helped run the counter. The second he saw Lys, he followed to her office. That habit of his was getting on her nerves.

She sat down in her swivel chair. "I'm surprised you're still here. Where's Magda?" She and another staff member served as assistant managers on alternating nights.

"I got a phone call that she's sick, so I stayed."

Lys was afraid she knew why. "That was good of you, but I'm here now so you can leave."

"Sometimes I don't feel like going back to an empty flat."

How well she knew that. "Tell me the truth. Do you wish you were home in Athens?"

"No," he answered almost angrily and moved closer to her desk.

"I hope you're telling me the truth. Now that I've taken ownership of the hotel, it's important to me that everyone is happy."

His eyes widened. "This hotel is *your* inheritance?"

"That's right."

She could see her revelation had completely thrown him.

"But you're so young—" *Whoa.* "I thought—"

"You thought Kyrie Rodino would have willed it to his ex-wife," she interjected. "That would have been a natural assumption. What else is troubling you?"

He hunched his shoulders. "Who's the mystery man?"

Lys decided it was time to set him straight and douse his hopes there could be anything between the two of them. She held out her left hand. He eyed it as if in disbelief.

"You can be the first on the staff to learn Takis Manolis asked me to marry him." What she would give if she could believe he truly did love her…

Giorgos's head jerked up. "How soon?"

"Aren't you going to congratulate me?"

"Of course," he muttered, then darted her a speculative glance. "I take it he knows you're the owner."

What was Giorgos thinking? Instead of answering him she said, "Thank you for going the extra mile to cover tonight, but you look tired. After putting in a full day's work already, you need to go home. I've let work pile up here and need to dig in. Good night, Giorgos."

Instead of indulging him further, Lys started scrolling through her messages until he left her office. After a half hour, she had cleared most of her work and after telling Chloe to call her if there was a problem, she went back to her suite to get some sleep. Not that it was possible with this incredible ring on her finger.

Takis phoned her Wednesday morning while she was drinking coffee in her room. "*Kalimera*, Lys."

Her heart thumped just to hear his deep voice. "How are you?"

"I'll be better when I see you later. At breakfast I told my parents I'd like them to meet you. They want us to come over to the hotel at two when business is slow."

Startled, she slid off the bed. "You mean today?"

"It surprised me too. My brother must have said favorable things about you. More than ever I'm convinced Danae was right about the engagement. My parents truly are anxious to see me settled." But they didn't know why Takis had asked her to marry him. "I'm leaving it up to you when you want me to come for you."

She glanced at her watch. "Where are you right now?"

"In my car on the way to the house. The water and electricity are supposed to have been turned on. I want to get over there and check things out."

"Then you have enough on your mind. I'm going to get ready and I'll take a taxi to your house."

"Lys—"

"No argument. I'll bring sandwiches and salad from the hotel kitchen." She rang off before he could try to reason with her.

Without wasting time, she called the front desk to let them know she was leaving the hotel. After hanging up, she showered, then washed and blow-dried her hair.

She didn't have to worry over what to wear and reached for her simple black gown she could dress up or down. It had sleeves to the elbow and a round neck. She wore tiny gold earrings and sensible black high heels.

When she was ready, she called the kitchen and gave them instructions. One of the waiters was to meet her at the hotel utility van in the garage with the food. Next she phoned the hotel florist. After telling them what she wanted, she asked that one of the employees bring the vase of flowers to the van and set it on the floor. After retrieving the flowers, she drove out to Tylissos.

It wasn't until she pulled up behind the two cars parked at the side of Takis's house that she realized there'd been a car behind her. She'd noticed it on the highway after leaving Heraklion, but it passed her by as she turned off the engine.

But seeing a hard-muscled Takis walk toward her drove every thought out of her mind and she trembled with excitement. Dressed in a casual cream-colored polo shirt and tan trousers, he was so striking, her breath caught.

"I've brought flowers," she said after he came

around to open the door. "I hope your mother will like them."

"It's a perfect gift."

"A woman can't resist flowers."

"I'll remember that." The way he eyed her made her pulse leap.

"They're on the floor in back."

He retrieved them while she brought the food and followed him into the house. But halfway through the living room she stopped because her eyes had caught sight of the fresco he'd rested on the mantel of the fireplace. The colors stood out, emphasizing the drabness of the room that needed a complete makeover.

He could see where she was looking. "I've been studying the fresco and think we need to pick one of the background colors that would look good on the walls."

She darted him a glance. "Do you have a favorite?"

"Yes, but I'd be interested to hear what you like."

"Well, I've loved this fresco for a long time and already know the one I'd use."

"In that case let's take it to the store and match the paint we want. I'll put these things in the kitchen and we'll eat later."

As she watched him disappear, Lys imagined that deep down he was anxious about introducing her to his parents and needed to keep busy. That was fine with her because her angst about being favorably received was shooting through the roof.

They went out to his car with the fresco and drove into the village. The thirtyish female clerk inside the store had them sit at a table. She couldn't seem to take her eyes off Takis even though she could see Lys wore an engagement ring.

After admiring the artwork, the woman set it on a chair before bringing in a dozen color strips for them to look through, but she addressed her remarks to Takis.

Though Lys knew Takis wouldn't be marrying her if Nassos hadn't given him half the hotel, she planned to help him redo his house. She adored him and wanted to help make it as beautiful as possible. This was where he planned to live until he died, so it had to be right.

His gaze fused with hers. "Let's pick our favorite color and see how close we come."

Being with Takis like this made every moment an exhilarating one. Among the various colors, her eye went to the pastel green shades until she found the perfect match in the fresco.

She would have reached for it, but Takis's hand was quicker. He lifted a certain strip off the table and glanced at her. "I knew exactly what I was looking for. Now it's your turn. Choose the one you prefer."

Lys couldn't believe it. "You're holding it. Soft sage is my choice too."

"You're teasing me."

"No."

The smile left his eyes. "I'm beginning to think we're dealing with something here beyond our control."

A little shiver raced through her. "I admit this is amazing."

"That was so easy, I'm afraid to ask what other colors you're thinking of for the rest of the house."

"How about these for the walls in the kitchen?" She picked up the Minoan red and canary yellow strips.

He looked astonished. "You've been reading my mind."

"The borders on the fresco influenced me."

Takis kissed her neck before getting up to talk to the clerk. He couldn't have done anything to please Lys more just then. She made a silent choice of pale blue for one of the bedrooms upstairs, but didn't say anything. Perhaps they'd make that decision later.

"I'll be happy to help you with anything else you need." The woman smiled into Takis's eyes and couldn't have been more obvious. Lys was glad to leave.

Again she thought she saw the same car she'd noticed earlier, but it disappeared around the next corner. After what she'd been through while the police were investigating the reason for Nassos's death, she was probably being paranoid.

CHAPTER EIGHT

SOON THEY DROVE back to the house with the paint. While Lys carried the bags into the living room, Takis brought in the fresco and set it back on the mantel. "Shall we eat? I'm starving."

Lys chuckled. "Aren't you always?"

They walked into the kitchen, where he'd put the wrapped vase of flowers in the sink earlier. She set the food on the table and they sat down to eat.

Halfway through a second sandwich he smiled at her. "We'll set up our computers to the hotel's mainframe. Giorgos won't be the wiser when we use this house to discuss business while we transform this place. Have you told him we're engaged?"

"Last night I showed him my ring."

Takis's eyes glittered with amusement. "It's the best thing that could have happened to him. He took one look at you and fell hard. I feel sorry for him because there's only one of you."

"Speaking of problems, maybe I should go alone to the paint store next time."

"Why?"

She laughed. "You do that so well."

"What?" He stared at her.

"Pretend you don't know that woman can't wait to see you again."

His mouth curved sensuously. "You noticed."

"Even blind, I would have been able to tell."

"Now you know what I put up with whenever you're with me. We both know Giorgos is already a lost cause. As for Basil, I've done business with him from time to time and have never known him to give anything away. But he was so besotted with my fiancée and her violet eyes, he lost his head."

She scoffed. "I thought he did it because he cares for you. More and more I'm convinced that's the way Nassos felt about you upon a first meeting, not to mention the manager, who was so impressed, he introduced you to Nassos twelve years ago."

He sucked in his breath. "Why do I feel I'm being set up for something?"

"Why don't you believe you're a wonderful son worth loving?"

They finished eating in silence before he started to clean up. "Thank you for bringing lunch." She felt his eyes on her. "We should leave for my parents' in a few minutes. If you need to freshen up, the water is on now. Don't worry. I cleaned the downstairs bathroom. This house has stood vacant for a long time."

"I thought as much."

She got up and discovered it next to the area for a washer and dryer down the little hall off the kitchen. There was a lot of work to be done, but Lys found she couldn't wait to help.

When she came out, he stood in the kitchen waiting for her. The realization of what they were about to do frightened her. "Takis? What if they can't accept me?"

"We've been over this before—they will adore you. Are you saying you want to back out?" His voice sounded too quiet.

"No, but I'm nervous."

His hands reached out and he drew her against him. "Perhaps now would be the best time to put the seal on our relationship." When his compelling mouth closed over hers, she'd been halfway out of breath in anticipation. The shocking hunger in his kiss robbed her of the rest and she clung to him in a wine-dark rapture.

There was no thought of holding back on her part. Her desire for him was so great, she had no idea how long they stood there clinging to each other, trying without success to satisfy wants and needs that had been kept in check until now.

"I've wanted you from the moment I saw you," he murmured, kissing every inch of her face and throat. "The desire we feel for each other is real. Don't tell me it isn't."

"I won't," she whispered, incapable of saying anything else.

Again he swept her away in another kiss that went on and on. His mouth was doing miraculous things to her. She couldn't bear the thought of this moment ending, but Takis had more control than she did and finally lifted his mouth from hers. His breathing had grown shallow too. "Much as I'm enjoying this, we're going to be late if we don't leave now."

She couldn't think, let alone talk, and was embarrassed for him to witness the state of her intoxication.

Needing to do something concrete, she pulled out of his arms and reached for the vase of flowers. After grabbing her purse, she headed for the living room.

He opened the front door and helped her out to his car. She hid her flushed face from him as much as she could for the short drive to the Manolis hotel. To her surprise he drove down an alley behind the buildings, parked by his parents' truck and came around to help her out.

"Are you ready?" he murmured.

She clung to the vase. What a question when her legs were wobbling! His kiss had changed her concept of what went on between a man and a woman now that she was so deeply in love with this fantastic man.

Of course she'd been kissed before and had enjoyed it, but she'd never gone to bed with the men she'd dated. During Nassos's talks with her about men and marriage, she'd learned that he expected her to wait until her wedding night. Maybe if she'd fallen in love with one of those men, she might not have been able to resist. But it hadn't happened and now she knew why after Takis had aroused her passion.

Suddenly the back door opened. Lys recognized his mother, who'd passed on her reddish dark-blond hair to Lukios. She cried Takis's name and reached out to hug him. But it was his same startling hazel eyes that fastened on Lys.

"Mama? This is my fiancée, Lys Theron. She's the light of my life." The words came out smooth as silk and sounded so truthful, it shook her to the foundations.

Lys looked for signs that she was upset or disappointed, but instead she let go of Takis to hug her, flowers and all. They were both the same medium height. "This is a great day. Welcome to the family."

The unexpected warmth brought tears to Lys's eyes. "Thank you, Hestia. Takis has talked about his angel *mama* so much, I feel I know you already." In that moment Lys shared an unexpected glance with Takis. From the intense look in his eyes, she'd said the right thing to his mother.

"She's brought you flowers. Shall we go inside and unwrap them?"

Hestia wiped her eyes. "Come on. Your father is in the living room waiting for you."

Nikanor Manolis. The man for whom this charade was all about.

Takis grasped her hand and took her through the kitchen to the living room.

Lys saw immediately that he took after his father in height and features. The older man with salt-and-pepper hair stood in front of the fireplace dressed in dark pants and a white shirt.

"*Baba?* I would like you to meet the woman I'm going to marry." Hearing those words almost gave her a heart attack. "Lys Theron, this is my father, Nikanor."

She shook his hand. "How do you do, Kyrie Manolis. It's an honor."

He gave her a speculative glance. "Lukios tells us you two met in Italy."

"Yes. I was on a short vacation."

"You love my son?"

After everything Takis had told her about his father, she guessed she wasn't surprised he would ask a blunt question like that. But Lys could hardly think for the blood pounding in her ears. "From the first moment I met him, I couldn't help it." She didn't dare look at Takis right then. To her surprise his father kissed her on both cheeks, putting his stamp of approval on the news.

"Look what she brought us!" Hestia came in the room carrying the vase of pink roses and lavender daisies, breaking the tension. "They are so beautiful!" She set them on the coffee table.

"I'm glad you like them. Those colors are perfect together."

"I think so too. Sit down. I've made tea."

Takis led her over to the couch and squeezed her hand, revealing his emotions. In a minute his mother came back with a tray of tea and *kourambiedes* to serve everyone.

"What are your plans?" his father asked.

"We've set the date for June fourth, provided that's a convenient time for you and Mama. It's not a holiday. The engagement announcement is ready to be given to the newspaper."

His father looked at Lys. His brows lifted the same way Takis's sometimes did. "Tell us about your family."

She'd been ready for that question. "My mother was an American, born on Long Island, who died when I was little. My father was working in New York, but he was from Kasos Island here in Crete. In his will he specified that he wanted his best friend to be my guardian should he die before I turned eighteen. That best friend was Nassos Rodino, who died very recently.

"He and his wife, Danae, raised me from the age

of seventeen after my father was killed in a plane accident. She's the only person I have left and still lives on Kasos. Contrary to what the media reported after his death, we love each other as mother and daughter and will always mourn Nassos's passing. He was like a father to me."

"We're sorry for your loss."

"Thank you. Danae met Takis for the first time the other night. When she learned he planned to live here for good and work at his family's hotel, she gave us her blessing. To be truthful, she never liked the men I dated. I'm pretty sure it's because they weren't from Crete."

Takis shot her a look of surprise.

"All along both she and Nassos insisted that one day I marry a Cretan who honors his family," Lys added on a burst of inspiration. It was only the truth.

The older man's gray eyes lit up before he turned to Takis. "That's what you want to do, my son? Work here at the hotel now that you're home for good?"

Lys's eyes closed tightly, waiting for the answer that would change Takis's world.

"It's what I want, *Baba*."

"Then so be it."

She knew those words had to be the sweetest Takis had ever heard.

"Hestia? They want to be married June fourth."

"I heard."

"In the Agios Titos church," Takis supplied.

"Ah. That's where we were married." Her face beamed. "How soon will it go in the paper?"

"We'll submit it tomorrow. It will probably show up the next day. We plan to see the priest next week."

His father nodded in what seemed like total satisfaction.

"When I'm not busy working for you, *Baba*, I'll be busy fixing up the old Andropolis house. You know the one that has stood vacant for close to a year. Besides paint, it needs new flooring and plumbing."

"You're good at those jobs."

A compliment from his father must be doing wonders for him, but Lys didn't dare look at him and instead munched on one of his mother's fantastic walnut cookies.

"We will have everyone for dinner Friday night to celebrate. Our whole family together."

If his mother had a serious illness, Lys couldn't tell. Nothing seemed wrong with Takis's father either. All she knew was that this get-together had to have left their son overjoyed.

Hestia moved over by Lys to examine the ring. "It doesn't surprise me he gave you the snake ring. My Takis was always immersed in our Minoan culture."

"I'm fascinated by it too. When he picked it up at Basil's, he also bought a replica of a fresco from the museum I admired. We're going to hang it over the fireplace and use those colors to decorate. You'll have to come and see it."

"I'll bring Kori and Doris with me."

"I'm looking forward to meeting them and the children."

"Everyone will be excited to get to know you. They love Takis and won't be able to wait to see his house."

"Takis will have to put up a railing on the upstairs terrace first so they won't fall."

"I'll take care of it before they come!" he spoke up,

as if they were an old married couple. She shouldn't have been surprised that he was listening.

Lys was getting in deeper and deeper. She loved him so much, but if he didn't love her just as intensely… While he kissed his father, Lys stood up, taking one more cookie from the plate. "These are so good, Hestia, I want the recipe."

"I'll give it to you."

In a moment Takis reached her side. "Mama, Lys and I need to leave so you two can get back to work. I'll be over for breakfast tomorrow and we'll talk hotel business."

She walked them out of the room and through the kitchen to the back of the hotel where the cars were parked. "Where do you live, Lys?"

"Since I started working in the accounts department of the Rodino Hotel four years ago, I've lived in a room there, but I've gone home to the island on weekends."

"Will you continue to work there when you're married?"

"I—I don't know." She hesitated. "Takis and I still have many things to talk about."

"Amen to that." He'd come up behind them. "We'll see you on Friday, Mama." He kissed her before helping Lys get in his car.

Hestia stood there smiling and waved as they drove down the alley to the next street.

"Your parents are wonderful," Lys murmured when they'd turned the corner.

He didn't respond. She turned her head toward him, waiting for him to say something. But he just kept driving until they arrived back at his house. Worried that something was wrong, she got out of the car and hurried toward the front door. In seconds, he'd unlocked it so they could go inside.

When it closed behind them, she felt his hands on her shoulders. He whirled her around. She couldn't understand the white ring outlining his mouth.

"Takis—" Her heart was thudding. "What did I do to make you this upset?"

"I'm not upset." He gave her a little shake. "Don't you know what you did back there was so miraculous, I'm afraid I'm dreaming."

Relief filled her system. "What do you mean?"

"You really don't get it, do you? You've charmed my parents so completely, you've made it possible for me to get in their good graces again."

She shook her head. "I didn't do anything. Can't you see how much they adore you?"

"That's your doing. You make me look good."

"What a ridiculous thing to say!"

"Ridiculous or not, you have my undying gratitude." His hands ran up and down her arms, bringing her against his hard male body. "Damn—we don't have a couch, let alone a bed, so I can't kiss you the way I want."

"It's probably a good thing there's no furniture."

"You don't really mean that." His deep grating voice sent waves of desire through her body. "I could eat you alive standing right here and know you feel the same way."

She took a deep breath. "I admit I've been strongly attracted to you from the beginning, Takis."

His gaze poured over her features relentlessly. "Have you ever been to bed with a man?"

"Would it matter to you if I had?"

"Yes," he bit out.

"Why? You've had intimate relations with other women."

A pained look crossed over his face. "I'm jealous of any man who has ever made love to you. I'd rather be the only one who knew that kind of joy."

"That works for women too."

"Are you admitting you're jealous of my past relationships?"

"Not jealous. But I do want to know about the one you had with your girlfriend in high school."

"We didn't sleep together, Lys. I was trying to honor her until we could be married."

Tears clogged her throat. "She was a very lucky woman to be loved by you. If the accident hadn't happened, you would never have left Crete and would probably be married with children by now."

"But destiny had something else in mind for me, and I'm in the battle of my life to regain what I lost."

She struggled to understand. "Tell me exactly what it is you think you lost. Your parents are thrilled you've come home and your father wants you working with him again."

His chest rose and fell visibly. "Because you're going to be at my side."

"You honestly believe it took *me* to make this happen today? If that's true, then I feel sorry for you."

Lines marred his striking features. "How else to explain why they want to tell the whole family Friday night?"

"How about accepting the fact that you're their son and they love you? Do you need more than that?

For so long you've been telling yourself that you're an unworthy son, you couldn't see what was in their eyes today. Why don't you just sit down with your father and tell him all the feelings in your heart?"

"My friend Cesare has asked me the same question."

"Then listen to him! Your fear has brought you to a standstill. For a man as outstanding and remarkable as you are, I find it inconceivable you're in such terrible pain. A simple conversation with your father could change the way you look at life." She lowered her head. "In a way, you remind me of Nassos."

Takis's head reared back. "What do you mean?"

"Remember the letter he wrote to me? Just think what might have happened if he'd gone to Danae and had admitted he'd been wrong to divorce her and wanted her back. But his fear that he might not be forgiven wouldn't let him do that and he died unexpectedly, never knowing how much she loved him and wanted to get back with him."

His brows furrowed. "How does that have anything to do with me?"

"It has everything to do with you. You're afraid to talk to your father for fear you'll hear him say he can never forgive you for leaving Crete. But the point is, he might say something else quite different to you.

"Just think, Takis. After my talk with Danae, I realized she would have told Nassos she wanted him back, but he never gave her a chance. It's so sad that it's too late for them. Please don't let it be too late for you and your father."

She kissed his firm jaw. "Now I'm going to leave and get back to the hotel. I've let work go too long.

When you're ready to start applying the primer, I'll come and help."

As she started out the door he said, "You still haven't told me if you've been to bed with a man."

She paused and turned to him. "Shall we make a deal? When you decide to have that talk with your father, then I'll tell you all the secret details of my intimate life with men."

"Was it true what you said about your boyfriends not being from Crete?"

"Yes."

"How many were there?"

"I only had three serious ones. All of them were born in other parts of Greece, the sons of wealthy parents who came to Crete for vacations and stayed at the hotel. I knew Nassos and Danae weren't impressed with any of them."

Her words brought a smile of satisfaction to his arresting features.

"By the way, I love your parents."

The next morning Takis made arrangements for a Skype conference call with his partners. He'd set up his computer in the kitchen while the guys sat at the computer in Cesare's office at the *castello*.

"You're looking good, amico." This from Cesare.

"It's great seeing you guys again."

"Before we hear your news, we have some of our own," Vincenzo exclaimed.

"Good or bad?"

"Definitely good. My cousin Dimi is going to marry Filippa in June at her church in Florence. They made the decision last evening, but want to keep it low-key with only family and close friends. You're invited, of course, if you can make it. We'll text you the time and address of the church."

Takis's mind leaped ahead. He would take Lys with him so his friends could meet her. Cesare had seen her, but it wasn't the same thing as talking to her. "I'm very happy for him. Dimi deserves it."

"Being that Filippa is Gemma's best friend, my wife is beyond thrilled. But now we want to know what's going on with you."

"Quite a lot actually. The sale of my hotels in New York has gone through. Furthermore I've bought myself a house two blocks from my parents' hotel in Tylissos and now have internet."

"You sound good."

"I am. Two days ago Lys Theron and I got officially engaged. Our announcement went in the newspaper today. I'm emailing you a copy of it as we speak."

After total silence, Cesare let out an ear-piercing whistle. "You're actually getting married?"

"We decided it was the best way to keep news about Nassos's will a secret. By implying that Lys and I are in a romantic relationship ending in marriage, no one will know or suspect I'm co-owner of the Rodino Hotel. She has informed the staff that she's the new owner."

Vincenzo leaned forward. "So what will you do? Get divorced after the six months' stipulation concerning hotel ownership has passed?"

"There'll be no divorce."

"Is she on board with all this?"

Takis had been waiting for Vincenzo's astute question, which meant his friend had been thinking hard about the things Takis hadn't explained. "I intend our marriage to last forever."

Cesare cocked his head. "The Takis I know wouldn't publicly announce his engagement to be married unless he wanted it more than anything else in this world."

"In the beginning I suggested the engagement in order to protect the relationship with my father. But I've fallen in love and yes, a life with her is what I want more than anything else in this world."

After a silence, "I take it you didn't have that conversation with him after all."

First Cesare, then Lys, now Cesare again. "I'm handling all I can for the moment. Any problems I need to know about business on your end?"

"Sofia, your assistant, might be getting married soon and will have to move back to Geneva," Vincenzo interjected. "That means we'll be needing to find a new person to replace her. Got anyone in mind?"

"Let me talk to her first. In the meantime I'll send Dimi a text to congratulate him."

"He'll like that."

"I know you guys are busy so I'll let you go."

"What's the hurry?"

"I'm waiting for a man to come and help me install a railing for the upstairs terrace on my house. You can't believe what a disaster this place is."

"Then we won't keep you. Ciao, Takis."

"Ciao, guys. It's always good to talk to you."

He ended the session and got back to work, purposely keeping their conference short. He knew they were worried about him and the rushed engagement. But he didn't want to let them delve into his psyche too deeply until Lys admitted that she was crazy in love with him too.

Once the wrought iron railing had been installed, he swept the stone tiles. Before long a truck from the local furniture store delivered a full-size swing with a canopy he'd ordered online.

The workers carried it upstairs to the terrace. They also brought up a round glass-topped table set in wrought iron with an umbrella and six matching chairs. There was also a matching side table he put next to the swing. Until the interior of the house was done, the terrace would be his hideaway with Lys. In the evening, the neighbors wouldn't be able to see them entwined.

After the men left, he phoned Lys. "How soon can the owner of the hotel come to my house this evening? I would pick you up, but I want to finish getting the primer paint on the walls by tonight. There's a surprise waiting."

"That sounds exciting. I'll be there as soon as I can with dinner." Click.

She did that a lot, cut him off so he wouldn't argue, but he found he liked everything she did. He was in love. The kind that went soul deep. One day soon he would get her to admit she couldn't live without him either.

CHAPTER NINE

AS LYS PULLED the van behind Takis's car at seven, she saw the surprise he'd mentioned. An attractive wrought iron railing with a motif of grapes and leaves had been installed on the terrace. He got things done so fast it was scary.

When she went inside, she was astounded to see Takis had put the primer on everywhere. It looked like a new house already!

She heard him call to her. "Come on up and bring the food!"

Lys needed no urging to dash upstairs. "Oh, Takis—this is fabulous!" she cried when she walked out on the terrace. It was even better than what she had imagined earlier.

He relieved her of the bags and put them on the table. She ran over to the swing and sat in the middle. "I love it!"

Takis followed her down so he was half lying on top of her. "So do I." He devoured her mouth until she was breathless. "I've been waiting for this since the moment I bought the house."

With his rock-hard legs tangled around hers and their bodies trying to merge, Lys had never known such euphoria. He was male perfection and she couldn't get enough of him. They lost track of time in their need to communicate.

"What if someone sees us?" she asked after coming up for breath.

"They won't. It's dark now, so I can do what I want." He bit her lobe gently.

"*Takis*—not here—"

"Are you afraid for us to make love?" He teased, kissing her throat.

"I thought that was what we were doing."

His deep laugh rumbled through her. "You say you had three boyfriends?"

She hid her face in his neck. "I did, but—"

"But it wasn't like this?"

Lys trembled. "We should eat. The food will be cold."

"Not until you tell me the truth. You've never been to bed with a man. Admit it."

"You're right. I haven't."

He kissed her with such tenderness, she couldn't believe it. "You have no idea how that changes my whole world."

"Why?"

"Nassos did the perfect job of protecting you so you could wear white to your wedding. Until we're married, I promise to honor his wishes for you."

She couldn't wait to lie in bed with him all night while they loved each other into oblivion. But what if he didn't love her the same way?

He kissed her lips once more. "You're so quiet. What's wrong?"

"Nothing," she muttered. Lys should never have admitted the truth.

"I think my fiancée is hungry."

"I think it's the other way around."

He gave her another deep kiss before standing up. "Come on." He reached for her hands. "Let's sit at our new table to eat."

After he'd set everything up he said, "I had a conference call with my partners this morning and there's news. We've been invited to Dimi Gagliardi's wedding in June. I don't know the exact date yet. He's Vincenzo's only cousin and one of my favorite people.

"He's marrying the best friend of Vincenzo's wife, Gemma, Filippa. We'll be flying to Florence for the ceremony."

"That sounds exciting."

He darted her a searching glance. "Now we have more important things to talk about. Next Tuesday evening the priest would like to meet us at the church."

Would he talk to the priest if he didn't love her? If he didn't want to marry her? She had to believe he meant what he said, but it was hard. "I think I'd better go. When I left the office, I still had some work to do."

He wiped his mouth. "In that case I'll follow you back to Heraklion and help you."

"I thought you didn't want to be seen."

"That was before our wedding announcement went in the newspaper. No one will think anything except that I'm so crazy about you, I can't stay away from you. For personal reasons, I want to make sure you get home safely. You're the most important person in my life."

No, she wasn't! Takis's father took priority, which was the reason they were in this situation now. Lys got up from the table and helped clean it off before going inside and down the stairs. Only a few minutes later, she had left the house and climbed into the van.

"Drive safely." He leaned in to kiss her hungrily. His touch caused her to melt before she turned on the engine and headed for Heraklion. Takis drove right behind her. At the hotel she parked the van and Takis parked in the empty space next to hers that Nassos had once used.

With his arm around her shoulders they took the elevator to the main floor and walked to her office. Along the way he kept her so close, anyone seeing them would assume they were lovers. By now the staff already knew.

Magda smiled her greeting before they disappeared down the hall to Lys's office. Takis walked her inside and pulled her into his arms. "I've got to have this before we do anything else."

She saw the blaze of desire in his eyes before he covered her mouth with his own, giving her a kiss that couldn't disguise his need. The slightest contact with him set her on fire and she found herself responding, helpless to do otherwise.

"We need a swing in here too," he whispered, kissing her eyes, nose, virtually every feature until he captured her mouth once more. "I'll arrange to have one sent from the store."

"*Takis—*" Lys finally found the strength to ease away from him. "I thought you wanted to help me work."

"I lied. Now that we're engaged, I don't want to be apart from you. I want you with me day and night."

"Please don't say that."

He caught her face in his hands. "Why? Because you know you want the same thing?"

"This is all happening so fast!"

His eyes gleamed like lasers. "That's not true. I saw you at the funeral and was determined to meet you the next time I came to Crete no matter what I had to do. Can you deny you felt something for me in my office in Italy?" he demanded before devouring her again.

Something in his tone convinced her he wasn't lying about his feelings. They'd both felt the chemistry between them when she'd flown to Milan. But a strong physical attraction didn't mean he loved her the way she loved him. Once they were married and he'd been reconciled with his father in his own mind, how would he feel then?

But for Lys, she'd never be able to love another man again. There was no one who came close to Takis. If their marriage didn't work out, she'd be like Danae and live a single life. With the money from her father, she could buy a place on Kasos near Danae. They could travel together, work on philanthropic projects together. But at this point the thought of Takis not being in her life was impossible to imagine.

"Lys?"

Startled, she tore her lips from Takis and turned her head to see Magda in the doorway.

"Sorry to intrude, but we have a problem."

"What is it? You can speak in front of my fiancé. Let me introduce you to Takis Manolis."

"It's very nice to meet you, Kyrie Manolis. Congratulations on your engagement."

"Thank you, Magda. I'm afraid you'll be seeing me around here a lot. I have a hard time staying away from Lys."

The other woman smiled before looking at Lys. "The finance minister Elias Simon from Athens has just checked in and was led to believe he could have the penthouse suite for the rest of the week."

Lys shook her head. "I can't imagine how that happened since we've never let guests sleep there. When Kyrie Rodino was alive, he used it for VIP meetings, nothing else. Tell the minister we'll put him in the Persephone suite."

"Will you tell him?" Her eyes pleaded with Lys, who understood her nervousness. Kyrie Simon had a forbidding presence.

"I'll take care of it."

"Thank you."

After she hurried away, Lys turned to Takis. "I'll be right back."

"I'll come with you."

The minute the two of them walked out to the front desk, the finance minister took one look and burst out, "Takis—"

"Elias—" The men shook hands.

"What are you doing here instead of New York? On business again?"

"I've moved back to Crete for good and got engaged." Takis grabbed Lys around the waist. "I'd like you to meet my gorgeous fiancée, Lys Theron, the former ward of Nassos Rodino. Now that he has passed away, she owns the hotel."

The other man's dark eyes fastened on her in male admiration and they shook hands.

"I envy you, Takis. If I were thirty years younger..."

"I'm a very lucky man."

"That certainly goes without saying," he said, smiling at her.

"Kyrie Simon? I'm sorry that there was a misunderstanding about the penthouse. It's not a guest room, but we'd love you to stay in the Persephone suite."

"No problem."

"Magda will check you in. Now if you will excuse me, I have some work to attend to back in my office."

"Of course. That gives me time to chat with Takis. You realize you're going to marry one of the most important men in the country. Has he shown you the hospital he built and funds in Tylissos? It provides such invaluable free medical care for the patients. There's another one being built in Athens as we speak. He's a remarkable man."

What?

"I'll tell you later," Takis said in an aside and kissed her cheek.

She went down the hall and sat down at her desk, but she couldn't concentrate on a thing. He'd built a hospital here? Another one was going up in Athens? How long had that been going on?

While she was alone, she phoned Danae, who was still awake. After catching her up on the latest news, she asked the older woman what she knew about a hospital in Tylissos that had been built and was free to the patrons.

"Only that it's a children's hospital for those parents who can't afford big medical expenses. Stella told me about it last year and wished the government would build one here in Heraklion."

Lys was stunned. "The government has nothing to do with it. I just found out tonight that Takis is the one who had it built and pays for everything."

A long silence ensued. "*Your* Takis?"

If only he were… She gripped the phone tighter. "Tonight Kyrie Simon, the minister of finance from Athens, checked into the hotel. He saw Takis. They appear to know each other well and it slipped out during their conversation."

"Your fiancé is a dark horse in many ways. What a lovely thing to find out about the man you're going to marry. If Nassos were still alive, he'd be bursting with pride."

"The man who should be overjoyed is his father, but I'm sure he doesn't know anything about all the great things his son has accomplished. It kills me that Takis lives with this terrible pain. I love him so much, Danae." They spoke a little longer before she hung up.

After another minute, Takis came back in her office. Her gaze fused with his. "I just got off the phone with Danae. Why haven't you told me about these hospitals?"

He stood in front of her with his legs slightly apart, so handsome, so masculine, she couldn't look away. "I would have gotten around to it."

"You told me your niece had to go to the hospital for an asthma attack. You had it built for *her*."

"For all children with medical problems whose parents struggle to make a decent living."

She shook her head. "But no one knows you were the one."

"I want it that way."

"Even your parents?"

"Especially them."

"But these hospitals aren't hotels. Your mother and father would be so thrilled and proud if they knew what you've done. And you're building another one?"

"I'd rather remain anonymous."

"Takis—they deserve to know more about your life!"

"They didn't deserve to be abandoned by their son."

Lys got to her feet, upset by his comment. "What can I say to convince you that they love you and never thought any such thing?"

His brows furrowed. "You can't. I'm sorry Elias let that information slip."

"I'm not. Don't you know how proud I am of you?"

"Thank you for that. But I know I can trust you not to say anything when we go to the family party tomorrow evening."

They weren't getting anywhere with this conversation. She took a deep breath. "Thank you for helping Magda out of a difficult situation. You've won her devotion." Takis had a rare potent male charm that had made mincemeat of Lys.

"It was my pleasure. Elias can be very intimidating. That's why he's in his particular position. Between us I think he makes the president of the country nervous."

Lys chuckled. "By tomorrow morning Magda will tell everyone that my fiancé is on first-name terms with a top-level Greek government official. You'll have elevated me to new heights in our staff's opinion."

His eyes narrowed on her mouth, sending darts of awareness through her. "Didn't you know it's the other way around? Elias insists on being invited to our wedding. He has a worse case on you than Basil. I didn't think that was possible."

She chuckled despite her out-of-control desire for him. "Don't be silly."

"Do you still have work to do, or shall I walk you to your hotel room?"

Lys wanted to be alone with him. She was bursting with feelings she was dying to share. "I'd like that." She grabbed her purse and left the room, turning out the light. They nodded to Magda and walked down the hall to the elevator. By the time they reached her suite, her heart was jumping all over the place.

Lys unlocked the door. "Come in."

"I'm afraid I can't."

She swung around in surprise. "Do you have to go right now?"

"Yes." Lines darkened his face.

"Why? Is something wrong at home?"

"No. The only problem is the way I feel about you. If I come in now, I'll make you my wife tonight and forget the ceremony. As it is, if I thought you'd say yes, I'd ask the priest to marry us in three weeks instead of three months' time."

Those words brought her close to a faint.

"Think about it and give me your answer tomorrow when I come to get you." In the next breath, he walked down the hall to the elevator, leaving her totally bereft.

She didn't want him to go. "Takis?"

He turned.

"Please don't leave yet."

"You'd better think hard about what you're asking. If I cross over your threshold, I won't leave till morning. Is that what you want after everything Nassos did to protect you from moments like this?"

For once in her life she was going to be honest and throw caution aside. "Yes."

"Why?"

"Because—because I need you and don't want to be alone tonight."

He moved closer, causing her heart to leap. "I need you too, but that's not a good enough reason to break all the rules."

"We've already broken several."

"But not the most important one."

"In my office earlier you said you wanted to be with me day and night."

"I do, once we're married."

His moral strength astonished her. "Nassos is no longer alive."

"Which leaves me to watch out for you. Weren't you the one who told me he probably gave me half ownership of the hotel to help keep you from making a mistake?"

"He didn't mean the kind of mistake we're talking about right now and you know it!" Her cheeks had grown warm. "You're going to make me say it, aren't you."

"Say what?" he murmured. "That you love me? That you can't live without me?"

The blood pounded in her ears. "You're a man who didn't plan to marry right away. I wonder what you'd do if I said those words to you."

His eyes gleamed an intense green. "Why don't we find out?"

He was toying with her, not helping her out. If he truly loved her, he wouldn't be so cruel. "To hear them would scare the living daylights out of you."

Takis cocked his head. "If you don't say them, we'll never know."

You're a fool, Lys. He was the most aggravating, incredible, beautiful man alive. "So you're really going to leave."

"It's your call. I dare you to sleep tonight, *agape mou.*"

Two words that meant beloved. *Was* she his beloved?

"*Kalinikta*, Lys."

"Good night!" she snapped at him in English.

She heard his chuckle clear down the hall until he disappeared. He was driving her crazy.

Takis, feeling pure joy, headed for the garage to get his car.

After saying good-night to Elias, he'd waited another couple of minutes outside Lys's office until she'd hung up from her phone call. He hadn't meant to eavesdrop, but it had been clear she'd been talking to Danae. That's when he'd heard the truth come from her own lips.

I love him so much.

Tomorrow evening they'd be with family and the

answers to all questions would come straight from their hearts. There'd be no deception, no regrets.

Early Friday morning Lys's phone rang. Excited because she knew who it was, she reached for her cell on the bedside table. "Takis?"

"No, Lys. It's Danae."

She sat up in bed. "What's wrong? You sound worried."

"If you haven't seen a newspaper or turned on television, then don't."

Alarmed by her words, Lys slid off the bed and got to her feet. "Tell me."

"The paparazzi have taken pictures of you and Takis together. One of the write-ups reads: 'Lys Theron, heiress to the Rodino fortune, sets her sights on marrying billionaire New York hotelier Takis Manolis. Is there nothing this gold digger won't do for money?'"

Lys's thoughts reeled. Though she'd been used to this kind of coverage after Nassos's death, she hadn't imagined that it would continue. How had the press discovered their relationship? Could it have been that car she had seen following her a couple of times. It must have been! But what concerned her was the impact it would have on Takis's parents.

"Thank you for telling me. I love you and am indebted to you. Now I've got to phone Takis and warn him in case he hasn't seen the paper yet." She hung up and rang him. *Pick up. Please pick up.*

To her chagrin the call went to his voice messaging. She left the message for him to call her immediately. Without hesitation, Lys took a quick shower and got dressed in a black sweater and skirt. Once she was ready, she hurried to the garage for her car.

Maybe he was painting and had turned off his phone. All she knew was that she had to find him. If the paparazzi were still following her, she didn't care. What mattered was tonight's get-together with Takis's family.

They would have seen or read this new barrage of sensationalizing information linking the two of them. Her desire to protect him from any pain had her pressing hard on the accelerator all the way to Tylissos.

Lys spotted his car at the house before she pulled up behind it. After getting out she ran to the door and knocked. When there was no answer, she tried opening it, but he'd locked it.

"Takis?" she cried out and knocked harder.

Maybe he was over at his parents' hotel. If Danae had seen the news, there was no doubt he'd seen it too. Possibly his brother might have come over to the house to talk to him and they were out somewhere. Or maybe he'd driven Takis over to the hotel.

She simply didn't know, but she intended to find out and dashed to her car. It didn't take long to reach the hotel. She parked near the front entrance and hurried inside. An attractive dark-haired woman manned the front desk.

"May I help you?"

Lys took a deep breath. "My name is Lys Theron. I need to speak to Takis Manolis. Is he here by any chance?"

"You're Lys!"

"Yes."

"I'm Doris, Lukios's wife."

"Oh—I'm so happy to meet you."

"We're all very excited about tonight."

If Takis's sister-in-law had seen the news this morning, she was hiding her reaction to it well.

"So am I, but I need to find Takis. Do you have any idea where he might be? I went over to the house and his car is there, but he didn't answer the door."

"Let me check with Hestia. She'll know." Lys waited while she made a phone call. When Doris hung up she said, "After breakfast he went to the village with his father and hasn't come back yet. If you'll wait just a minute, she's going to phone him and find out when he'll be back."

Lys held back her groan. "Thank you." The poor darling was probably trying to defend her reputation the best way he could, but it didn't look good.

Doris's phone rang and she picked up. Their conversation didn't last long before she clicked off. "They may be gone for a while. Hestia would like you to come back to their apartment. She wants to talk to you. Their door is at the end of the left hall."

"I appreciate your help, Doris."

Shaking inside as well as out, she headed for the apartment where Takis had been born and grew up. Hestia met her at the door with a hug and asked her to come into the living room. Wonderful smells from the kitchen filled the room.

"I'm sorry to come by now when I know you're preparing for this evening, but I need to see Takis as soon as possible."

His mother eyed her with concern. "Something's wrong. What is it?"

She sat on the couch, folding her arms against her waist. "I wish I could tell you."

"If it's about the latest tabloid gossip, I pay no attention to it."

Lys let out a slight gasp. "Then you know what was in the paper this morning."

"Takis mentioned it at breakfast before he and his father left the hotel together."

"I went over to his house, but he's not there. I—I'm so afraid."

"What is it?" she asked in such a kind voice, Lys had to fight the tears that threatened. "He asked me to marry him, but I fear I'm not the right kind of woman for him. That's what I need to tell him so we can call off this engagement party."

"My son has never done anything he didn't want to do. He wants you for his wife."

"But gossip follows me wherever I go and it will rub off on him. I'd do anything to protect him and your family."

"Tell me something truthfully. Do you love him?"

Her question brought the tears rolling down her cheeks. "Desperately, but he loves you and your husband with all his heart. He's been so traumatized all these years for hurting you by leaving Crete, the last thing he needs now is to marry a woman who will bring more hurt to you."

His mother shook her head. "What hurt are you talking about?"

Lys wiped her eyes. "He carries this terrible guilt that he abandoned you when he left for New York. He can't forgive himself for it."

"Oh, my dear—" She came over to the couch and

put her arm around Lys. "By the time Takis was a year old, his father and I knew he was different than the other two. He insisted on exploring his world and needed more to make him happy. When his girlfriend died, we knew he had to find his life and were thrilled that Kyrie Rodino gave him that opportunity."

"You were?" Lys cried. "Honestly?"

"Of course. We're so proud of what he's done and accomplished."

Lys couldn't comprehend it. "Then he's the last person to know. He's been afraid that he's let you down and can never win your approval. And he's worried that there's—" She stopped herself before she said something she shouldn't.

"That there's what?" Hestia prodded.

"If I tell you, I'm afraid he'll never forgive me."

"Of course he will."

"H-He's afraid either you or your husband are seriously ill," her voice faltered. "He thinks that's why you asked him to come home for good."

His mother lifted her hands in the air. "We're in the best health we can be at our age."

"Oh, thank heaven!" Lys half sobbed.

"Where would he get an idea like that?"

"Because you asked him to come home. He thought there had to be a vital reason."

"There was. There is. We love him, and we miss him. We figured he'd made enough money on his hotels that he could come back and do something else amazing here in Crete."

"He has done that!" Lys jumped to her feet. "You know the children's hospital where your granddaughter had to go the other day?"

Hestia nodded.

"Takis had that hospital built and funds it completely." At this point tears spilled down his mother's cheeks. "He's building another one in Athens."

"Our dear son," she whispered.

"Please, Kyria Manolis. Let him know how you feel. Tell him you're both healthy. Reassure him you wanted him to find his way in the world. He needs to know how much you love him so he'll be whole. But he doesn't need a woman with my reputation ruining his life. Forgive me, but I don't dare marry him." She removed her ring and handed it to Hestia. "Please give this to him. Now I have to go."

Hestia called to her, but she dashed out of the apartment to her car. The tears continued to gush as she drove toward Heraklion. Her phone rang, but she didn't answer it. When she reached the hotel, she parked the car and rushed to her suite.

Once inside, she ran sobbing to her bedroom and buried her face in the pillow. When her phone rang again, she refused to answer it in case it was Takis. If he knew what she'd done by confiding in his mother, then he might never want to speak to her again.

Takis was surprised when his mother met him and his father at the back door of the apartment. "I'm so glad you're home! Your fiancée has been trying to reach you."

"I know. I tried to call her back, but she hasn't answered yet."

"I'm not sure she's going to."

He frowned and followed her inside to the kitchen. "What do you mean?"

She glanced at his father. "Both of you need to sit down so we can talk."

Takis lounged against the counter, unable to sit until he knew what was going on.

"Lys came by the hotel earlier looking for you."

Takis groaned aloud. "We went into the village to pick up the bedroom furniture you ordered and set it up at the house. I wanted it to be a surprise for her."

His mother nodded. "While you were busy, we had a very informative talk about many things including the children's hospitals you've been building. I'll tell you everything, but first I want you to know you're the luckiest man on earth to have found a woman who loves you so much."

"She admitted that to you?" Takis was stunned.

"You'd be shocked what she told me." In the next breath she related their whole conversation, leaving nothing out. After she'd finished, his father spoke first.

He stared at Takis through eyes that glistened with tears. "Your mother and I have loved you since the day you were born. We were so afraid for you after Gaia's death, we rejoiced when Kyrie Nassos opened a new door for you. We didn't want to say or do anything to discourage you from leaving, and we've never regretted that decision. You have no idea how proud we are of you."

Takis couldn't believe what he was hearing. Cesare had been right about everything. As for Lys…

"We're not ready for the grave yet, son. We expect to enjoy years of life with you and the wonderful woman who loves you enough to have confided in your mother."

Takis was so overcome with emotion, he could only hug them for a long time. After clearing his throat, he said, "Since Lys was so honest, I have something important to tell you too. You may not love me so much when you hear what I've done. It's about the reason we're engaged. Nassos left a will."

Once his whole confession was out, silence filled the room. His father walked over and clapped him on the shoulder.

"I only have one thing to say. The fact that Kyrie Nassos thought so much of you he would give you half his hotel tells me and your mother that you're the finest, most honorable Manolis we've ever known. I think all that's left to say now is that you go find your fiancée and thank her for making this family closer than ever."

His mother smiled. "I already love her." She reached in her apron pocket and pulled out the engagement ring. Takis was aghast Lys had taken it off. "Give it back to her with our love."

Takis's heart was running away with him. He looked at his father. "Will you drive me home so I can get my car? I need to go after her before she decides to do something crazy like leave the country."

"Where would she go?"

"To a friend of her mother's in New York. If that's her plan, I've got to stop her."

Takis broke all speed records driving into Heraklion. It was a miracle he wasn't pulled over. To his relief, her car was still in its space when he parked his Acura. But she could have called for a limo. There wasn't a moment to lose.

He hurried to her suite and knocked on the door. When she didn't answer, he phoned her. Still no response. Without a second to lose, he raced to the front office. Magda was on duty.

"Have you seen Lys this afternoon?"

"No."

"She hasn't left the hotel?"

"Not that I know of. Let me check with the manager." She came right back. "No one has heard from her."

"Then I need a card key to her room. I'm worried about her. We're due at our engagement party."

Magda seemed hesitant.

"Tell you what. Will you come with me and let me in?"

"Yes." She grabbed a card key. Then she turned to the other woman manning the desk and said she'd be right back. Together they hurried to the third floor.

Magda knocked on Lys's door and called out to her. After no response, she used the card key to let them inside.

"Lys?" Takis called her name. "It's Takis. Are you ill?"

"What are you doing inside my suite?" sounded a familiar voice in an unfamiliar tone. He could rule out sickness. Her voice sounded strong.

Relief flooded his system that she hadn't gone anywhere yet. He thanked Magda. "I'll take care of this now. I promise you're not in any trouble."

"I'll have to take your word for that."

After she left, he started down the hall. "I'm coming in the bedroom, so if you're not decent, you'd better hide under the covers."

"I'm dressed if that's what you mean."

He moved inside. She looked adorable sitting on the side of her bed in a pink robe and bare feet, her face splotchy from crying.

Her purple eyes stared accusingly at him. "How did you get in here?"

"I'm part owner of the hotel, remember?" He sat down on a side chair.

"Nobody knows that."

"Magda let me in."

"Of course she did once you used your charm on her. She should be fired!"

"On the contrary, she passed the most important test for me by functioning in a crisis."

"What crisis?"

"I couldn't find you anywhere. After the talk with my mother, I feared you might be in here too ill to respond. In my opinion we should make Magda general manager if Giorgos ever leaves."

Lys lowered her head. "Then your mother told you everything."

Takis loved this woman with every atom of his body. "Yes."

She got to her feet. "The headline in the paper has probably ruined everything you've tried to do where your father is concerned. For all I know it already has."

"You couldn't be more wrong."

Lys paced the floor, then turned to him. "Why didn't you answer your phone this morning?"

"I was out shopping for our bedroom furniture with my father and turned it off."

Lys blinked. "You went with your father to do that?"

"Yes. It's tradition for the parents. He insisted and we had a lot of fun."

"Then it means he didn't see the paper this morning."

"True, but *I* did, and I told my parents about it at breakfast."

He heard her take a quick breath. "Did your mother tell you I've broken our engagement?"

"Yes." He reached in his pocket and pulled out the ring. "Here's the proof. It would have been nice if you'd told me first."

"I did try, but you weren't anywhere around."

"We've got all the time in the world now."

"You don't need an explanation. We both know we can't go on with this lie any longer. It's not fair to your parents who love you."

"What lie is that?"

"The only reason two people should get married is because they love each other. Your parents have to know the real reason we got engaged. But since you don't want them to know about the will, I can't go on with this deception."

"You don't have to. They know about it."

He could see her swallowing hard. "When did they find out?"

"I told them this afternoon."

She sank down on the end of the bed. "I don't understand."

Takis got to his feet. "I finally had the talk with them you urged me to have. You were right about everything and I was wrong. When I explained about the will, they told me they were thrilled Nassos thought enough of me to give me such a gift."

"Oh, Takis—" she cried, sounding overjoyed. "Then there are no more shadows? You're happy at last?"

"No. I'm still waiting for you to tell me if you love me. The other night you wanted me to stay with you. An admission of love would have brought me running to you."

She looked away from him. "You're being very unkind, Takis. After talking to your mother, you *know* I do."

"You do *what*?"

"Love you."

"When did you know?"

"In your office in Italy. But none of it matters because a love like mine needs to be reciprocated, which it isn't, so I wish you'd leave now."

"I can't do that because I love you more than life."

A gasp escaped her lips. She turned to him. "I don't believe you," she whispered.

"Do you honestly think I would have asked you to marry me if you hadn't turned my world inside out? I knew at the funeral you were the woman for me. The moment was surreal to watch my destiny walk past me. The feeling I had for you transcended the physical. How can you doubt it?"

"Because I'm afraid to believe it."

He reached for her left hand and slid the ring back on her finger. Then he cupped her beautiful face in his hands. "I can understand that fear. You lost your parents and Nassos. But you're never going to lose me. We're going to get married and raise a family."

She wrapped her arms around his neck. The love-light in her eyes blinded him. "I love you so much I don't think I can contain it."

"I don't want you to try." Driven by desire, he picked up his bride-to-be and carried her over to the bed, following her down on the mattress. "If you had any idea how long I've been waiting to love you like this. Give me your mouth, my love."

Her passionate response was a revelation to Takis, but they'd no sooner started kissing each other than her cell rang, followed by a loud knock on the hotel room door.

He was slow to relinquish her luscious mouth. "I'll get the door while you answer the phone."

When he hurried down the hall and opened it, he discovered Danae standing in the hallway, the phone in her hand.

A smile broke out on her face. "I'm relieved you're the reason Lys hasn't answered her phone."

He reciprocated with a smile of his own. "I'm relieved it's you instead of the manager. Come in. She'll be thrilled to see you."

Danae kissed him on the cheek. "Liar," she whispered.

Lys came hurrying into the living room and gave Danae a hug. "I'm sorry I didn't answer the phone earlier."

"That's all right. I'm thinking you two need to move up the wedding date. How about three weeks from now? Check with your parents. We'll have the reception on Kasos."

Takis had never known this kind of happiness.

"You're a woman after my own heart, Danae. Since you're here, I'm going to leave."

Lys darted him a beseeching glance. "Do you have to go?"

This was like déjà vu. Luckily Danae had interrupted them, preventing him from breaking his vow not to make love to her before the wedding.

"Yes." She knew the reason why. "I'll be back later to take you and Danae to our engagement party." He gave her a brief kiss on the mouth before letting himself out.

CHAPTER TEN

Three weeks later

THE DAY BEFORE the wedding, Takis's close friends flew in from Milan. While the men met together, Gemma, Vincenzo's wife, and Filippa, Dimi's fiancée, came to Lys's hotel room to talk. Lys was delighted to get acquainted with the two women, who were best friends and so important in Takis's life.

It was clear to her they were all going to become close, especially when Gemma announced that she was pregnant.

"Does Vincenzo know?"

She smiled at Lys. "Oh, yes, and now he's so excited and worried over my morning sickness, he never leaves me alone. The doctor gave me an antiemetic and now it's under control, but Vincenzo has been driving me crazy. If he behaves like this until the baby is born, I might lose my mind."

"No, you won't," Filippa quipped. "He won't allow it."

Lys couldn't stop laughing. "Do you think your doctor will let you go on in your position as executive pastry chef?"

"I've already talked to my ob about that. He's monitoring me carefully and will tell me when it's time to quit. Vincenzo and I have already talked to Cesare, who is in the process of looking for a replacement."

"I don't know," Lys murmured. "Takis says you walk on water."

"She does," Dimi's fiancée concurred.

Gemma grinned. "Stop it, you two. There are plenty of great cooks out there and there's still plenty of time." She eyed Lys. "I'm so excited for you and Takis. He's the most gorgeous, wonderful man. He'll move mountains for you because it's the way he's made."

"I knew that about him before we even met and was halfway in love with him sight unseen."

"You really never met him when he was working in New York?" Filippa couldn't believe it.

"No. I was a sixteen-year-old high school student when he first started working for my father and I was hardly ever at the hotel. A year later my father died and Nassos brought me to Crete."

"Takis's story is an incredible one. So is yours," Gemma murmured. "I'm so glad you'll be spending some time at the *castello* after your honeymoon. Takis loves it there."

Gemma nodded. "We can't wait to all be together. The men have missed him more than you can imagine, Lys. You have to promise you'll fly to Milan often or life won't be the same around the place."

"It's true," Filippa said with a smile. "Dimi looks upon him as a brother. They're all so close."

"I think it's very touching," Lys murmured.

"In case you didn't know, that man can't wait to

marry you. Dimi says if he has to wait one more day, he's not going to make it."

"I feel the same way."

"We can tell." Gemma chuckled. "Since we've been given our specific instructions, we'd better hurry out to the limo to meet the men."

"They're taking us to lunch," Filippa informed Lys. "We don't dare be late or Vincenzo will come charging in here to find out what's wrong with Gemma."

Laughter broke out as they made their way down to the lobby. Lys hadn't known what it was like to have a sibling. Now she felt she'd acquired several for life.

The next day Lys stood before the black-robed priest dressed in floor-length white silk and lace. She carried a sheaf of purple roses that matched the genuine purple sapphire earrings Takis had given her as a prewedding gift.

During their midmorning wedding ceremony at the flower-decked church in Heraklion, surrounded by their families and a few close friends, Lys was in a complete daze.

The sight of Takis, her tall Cretan prince in his dark blue suit and wedding crown, pushed everything else out of her mind. That picture of him would be engraved in her thudding heart forever. He was now her husband, the most wonderful, gorgeous man in the entire world!

As they were led in the walk around the table three times where they drank from the cup, signifying their journey through life together, she prayed you couldn't die of happiness. By keeping his vow to her, he'd made this sacred moment meaningful in a way nothing else could have done. But now that she was his wife, she couldn't wait to show him what he meant to her.

They would be spending time on the yacht Danae had offered them, but where they were headed was a secret. Every time she thought about their wedding night and being alone with him, waves of desire swept through her. Once they left the church, she was scarcely cognizant of their helicopter flight to Kasos for the reception.

Danae had outdone herself to make Takis's family and friends comfortable. She'd arranged for every one of them to stay overnight where they could swim and eat and enjoy this wedding holiday.

What delighted Lys most were the three children who adored their uncle Takis and hung around the two of them. The girls touched her dress and veil and asked dozens of questions.

Deep inside Lys hoped she'd get pregnant soon. When she saw how happy he was teasing them, playing with them, that day couldn't come soon enough. The second bedroom upstairs would make the perfect nursery when the time came and she knew the color she wanted.

In the midst of the excitement, Takis's father stood to make a toast. "I'm the proudest of men to see my last remarkable child married to a lovely woman who I hope will do her Cretan duty and provide us with more grandchildren." He'd read Lys's mind.

Takis gripped her hand and clung to it.

After Nikanor's toast, Dimi stood up. "I couldn't love Takis more if he were my own brother. I'm thrilled he married a woman I already love. Lys has accomplished something no one else could ever do by putting the light in his eyes that was missing."

"It's true," Takis whispered against her ear.

Lukios followed with a toast. "Guess what, Dimi? I *am* blood and couldn't be prouder of my remarkable brother, whose greatest achievement is sitting next to him. Welcome to the family, Lys."

She teared up while other toasts followed. Eventually Cesare raised his glass of champagne. "Here's to the groom, a man who kept his head even while he lost his heart. I was there at the *castello* the day he lost it and witnessed the earthshaking event with my own eyes."

Everyone roared, especially Takis, whose laughter told Lys it was a private joke between the two of them. She'd have to ask him about it later.

Then Vincenzo gave the final toast and lifted his glass. "Here's to the newest Manolis couple on Crete. Like my beloved wife and me, may they remain lovers for all of life and the hereafter."

"You can plan on it!" Takis declared without shame, causing everyone to laugh and clap. Then he pressed a kiss to her cheek. "It's time for you to change. We're taking a helicopter ride to the yacht. Hurry. I can't wait to get you alone."

Those words said in his deep voice charged her body and she left for her bedroom to put on the stylish new cream-colored suit she and Danae had picked for her. She pinned a purple rose corsage to the shoulder. It was heaven to be out of mourning at last. The sorrow of the past was gone. With Takis waiting for her, there was nothing but joy ahead.

Twenty minutes later everyone followed them outside to the helicopter. Twilight had crept over them. Lys hugged Danae, both of them shedding happy tears. "I have no doubt your parents and Nassos were looking on today."

A sob caught in her throat. "I think so too. I love you. Thank you for everything and for making his family and friends so welcome. We'll be back soon."

"You've married a very exciting man, Lys. I envy you for what's in store."

Lys watched Takis hug his family before he helped her climb on board and told the pilot they were ready. Earlier in the day their luggage had already been flown out.

Lys was thankful they didn't have to fly a long distance. She'd anticipated this moment too long to wait any longer. Before she knew it, they'd put down on the landing pad of the yacht. She practically leaped out of her seat, anxious to be alone with Takis who helped her out.

"Am I dreaming, darling?"

He stopped to kiss her thoroughly. "If you are, I'm in it with you. *Forever.*"

Their wedding night was about to begin. Now if her heart would stop running away with her, she might be able to breathe.

When they reached the outer doors of the master cabin, he swept her in his arms and carried her over the threshold. "At last," came his fierce whisper.

"*Takis—*"

His friends had prepared the suite to his specifications. The flower-laden room was lighted solely with candles. Bless Danae for confiding in him about Lys's fascination with the prince in the fresco. Not only had she told him there was a strong resemblance to Takis, but Lys had once said that in a fairy-tale world, she would love to be married to the prince.

Upon hearing that, Takis had made up his mind that on their wedding night, he'd treat her like a princess. He couldn't re-create a Minoan palace, but he would convince her she was the most precious thing in his life. As he lowered her to the floor, adrenaline gushed through his veins in anticipation of what was to come.

Her heart kicked her ribs hard as she looked around, leaving him to freshen up in the bathroom. She'd been on this yacht many times before, but rarely came in this room and had never seen it looking like this. Takis had transformed it into a bridal chamber fit for a queen. The perfume from the flowers was intoxicating. She walked over to smell the ones next to the bed.

"Takis?"

"I'm right here."

She turned to him and almost fainted. He looked so beautiful in the simple white terry cloth robe, she couldn't think, let alone talk. His eyes gleamed like green gemstones in the soft light.

He handed her an identical robe. Her knees came close to buckling. With hands that were trembling, she went in the en suite bathroom. After removing her clothes, she put it on.

Lys had known he had a creative side to his nature, but to go to this kind of trouble to please her endeared him to her in a brand new way. With her heart beating out of control, she walked back into the bedroom.

He stood at the side of the massive bed. "Come closer so I can look at the most beautiful bride in all Crete."

"Takis—"

"You're not frightened of this surely? Not after all we've been through."

"I—I don't know what I am," her voice faltered.

"You're my desirable wife, the compassionate-hearted woman I've wanted from the moment I first laid eyes on you. I don't deserve you, but I swear an oath that I'll love you forever. Come here to me, *agape mou*."

She flew into his arms. He swung her around before lowering her to the bed. Their mouths met in frantic need and they began to feast on each other. One robe, then the other landed on the floor.

Their bodies came together in an explosion of love and desire. Lys hadn't known it could be like this. All night long they gave and received unimaginable rapture. "I love you so much, Takis. You just don't know..."

"Then you have some concept of how I feel. You're the light of my life, Lys. Love me, darling, and never stop."

They didn't stop. It wasn't till midmorning there was a loud knock on the cabin door.

Lys groaned and held him tighter. "Tell whoever it is to go away."

"If it wasn't for the fact that Cesare prepared our breakfast before leaving, I would. But he's sure to have given explicit instructions to make sure that we ate a perfect Cretan breakfast."

A chuckle escaped her lips. "And he knows how

hungry you are for every meal. I love him for that since I forgot all about feeding you."

He kissed a certain spot. "You've fed me the nectar of the gods, but it's true I still need mortal food and his creations are out of this world. In truth he should be the new cook for the restaurant after Gemma leaves."

"Have you told him that? Maybe he'd like to do it for a while."

"I'll have to run it by Vincenzo. Do you know Cesare had always said his mother was the best cook who ever lived?"

"That's a thought. We'll have to talk some more about it, but right now I know you're hungry. So am I." She kissed his hard jaw that needed a shave and let him go long enough to slide out of bed and put on her robe. "Stay there and I'll get it."

He lay back on the pillows, looking every inch the prince of her dreams. There wasn't enough she could do for him. "I love you desperately, Takis, and want to do everything I can to make you happy."

After kissing him passionately, she flew across the room. A staff member had left the tray with Cesare's breakfast beside the door. It was laden with every conceivable dish Takis would love. She carried it to their bed, where they could lounge and eat to their hearts' desire.

After eating as much as she could, she lay back. "You're right. I've never tasted better food in my life." She eyed her fabulous husband. "Would it hurt his feelings if you actually approached him with the idea of being the chef at the hotel in Milan?"

Takis put the tray on the floor, then pulled her back

in his arms. "Of course it wouldn't," he murmured against her throat. "After running his own chain of restaurants in New York, he's been begged by restaurants around the world to be their executive chef. All he has to do is name his price."

She covered his face with kisses. "But he wants to be with you and Vincenzo and Dimi. You four have an amazing relationship. I'd be jealous if I didn't understand how it all started, and why."

"We're very close, but you will always come first."

"Why did you laugh so hard when Cesare made his toast?"

"I was afraid you would ask." He kissed her again. "After you left my office, he witnessed my meltdown. I couldn't understand why Nassos had left me half a hotel.

"To make matters more complicated, I'd just met you after seeing you at the funeral. Since then you'd never been out of my thoughts and I knew in my soul *you* were the woman meant for me. But I didn't want to be in love. At the height of my frustration, I threw the deed across the room, but it landed on Cesare's chest."

She burrowed her face in his neck, chuckling quietly. "Thank you for telling me. You have no idea how much I love you." Her eyes filled. "It was the perfect wedding, wasn't it?"

"Almost as perfect as you. Thank God for Danae giving me her blessing. And thank God for Nassos for bringing us together. If I didn't know better, I could believe he had an inkling that he might not be on this earth long. Every time I think about his letter to you and the deed to me, I get a prickling down my spine."

"So do I," she said in a shaken voice. "I—I can't imagine life without you now."

"Don't try. I'm planning to love you all day and night for the rest of our lives, Kyria Manolis."

She smiled and kissed him with fervor. "That's right. I *am* Mrs. Manolis, and I want a baby with you as soon as possible. The next time we go to the paint store to pick out the color for the nursery, *I* plan to be the one that woman deals with, not you. I want blue."

"I was thinking pink."

They kissed again. "For once we disagree."

"No. We'll simply build another couple of rooms on the rear of the house. I'd like to call our first daughter Lysette, in honor of Nassos. He brought us together, my love."

"That's so sweet." She covered his face with kisses. "Spoken like my unmatchable husband. I think our first boy should be Nikos Takis Manolis, in honor of your father and *you*!"

Takis's low chuckle melted her bones before he rolled her over and began kissing her into oblivion.

Much later they were served another exquisite meal. After they were replete, Takis lay on his side so they could look into each other's eyes. "I have an idea what we should do with the hotel in Heraklion."

"So do I. We'll keep it and run it together."

"Yes, and whichever one of our children shows an interest in running it, we'll let them have at it."

She traced his lips with her finger. "What if one of them wants to change it in unorthodox ways? How will you feel about that?"

He took a deep breath. "One thing is for sure. All of us will talk everything out together so there can be no chance for misinterpretation that can lead to years of uncertainty."

"Oh, I'm so glad you said that!" she cried. "No woman was ever so lucky. Come here, my husband, and let me love you like you've never been loved before. I might not let you out of this room for days."

"I'm going to hold you to that promise, you beautiful creature."

By the first of June the weather was actually hot in Florence, Italy. Lys had felt sick before they'd flown here and had welcomed the cool of Dimi's villa.

Either her symptoms meant she was coming down with the flu, or… *Was it possible she was pregnant this soon?* Gemma had confided that she'd had similar symptoms when she realized she was carrying Vincenzo's baby.

Before leaving for the church the next morning, Lys did a home pregnancy test. To her joy, it showed she was pregnant with Takis's baby. But she didn't want to tell him the news until after Dimi's wedding.

The festivities leading up to the big day and exquisite marriage ceremony had worn her out and after they left for Dimi's villa following the reception, she noticed the temperature hadn't cooled down.

For the moment, she longed to lie down in their room until their flight home tomorrow. But once they were in the limo, Takis told the chauffeur to drive them to the airport. She turned to her husband in alarm. "I thought we weren't leaving until tomorrow."

He flashed her his mysterious smile. "Don't worry. I made arrangements for our luggage to be put on the plane. We're taking a little twenty-four-hour detour to Milan before we go home. After our honeymoon on the yacht several months ago, I wanted us to enjoy another one in Milan, but decided to save this surprise until after Dimi's wedding."

She hated to tell him she wasn't feeling well and spoil his plans. "I—I didn't realize you have work to do at the *castello* this trip," her voice faltered. All she wanted was to get back to the villa and go to sleep in a cold room, but he'd been so wonderful to her, she couldn't dampen his happiness right now. With Dimi's marriage, he was on a high.

Takis kissed her. "This isn't for work. Humor me, *agape mou.*"

She loved him so much she would do it if it killed her.

Two hours later when they pulled up to the front entrance parking, he kissed her awake. "Come on, sleepyhead. We're here."

She tried her best to cooperate as they walked up the endless stairs leading to the main entrance. He hurried them inside and down the hall to the rear of the *castello,* where she had to face a winding stone staircase.

Her head began to swim as they ascended the medieval tower, and positive she wouldn't make it, she sagged against him.

"Are you all right? We're almost there."

"My darling husband—are you sure you don't hope I'll expire before we reach the top?"

The whole shadowy medieval stairway echoed with his laughter. "A few more minutes and all your fears will disappear."

When she reached the fortress-like door, he opened

it for her. "We've arrived where it will be my joy to wait upon my precious wife."

Her heart kicked her ribs hard as they walked over the threshold and he led her toward the bedroom. The tower suite was a vision of ducal elegance dating back several centuries. The light through the stained-glass windows covered the room in thousands of different colors and nearly took her breath away.

"Takis?"

"Go ahead and lie down on the bed. I'll be right back."

It was heaven to take off her suit and just sink onto the bed. She had no strength at this point. A minute later she heard him call to her and she opened her eyes.

Lys didn't know what to expect, but it wasn't to see the prince of her dreams come to life before her eyes. He looked so magnificent in the white tunic, and in the dimly lit room, Takis's eyes gleamed from his bronzed face.

In spite of how ill she felt, Lys's heart began to beat in time with the desire that thrummed through her veins and she tried to sit up, but he sank down on the massive bed next to her.

"Don't move. I want to look at my beautiful wife."

"Takis—"

"Since the moment you became my wife, since the moment I met you, I knew that you were the one person I needed, the one person I loved. I swore on our wedding night that I'd love you forever. And I intend to show you just how seriously I take that oath. Come here to me, darling."

But as he lowered his mouth to kiss her in frantic need, she had to turn away from him.

"Lys—are you all right?"

"I'm fine," she cried gently. "It's just that... I'm not feeling too good."

He smoothed his hand against her cheek. "I had no idea you felt ill. You should have told me."

"It's been coming on for a couple of days. I didn't want to say anything."

"I'm sending for the doctor." Anxiety had wiped the glow from his face and eyes. It reminded her of the way Vincenzo had looked at Gemma, who'd suffered serious morning sickness in the beginning of her pregnancy.

"No. It's all right. I don't need a doctor. I took a test."

"A test?" Takis looked at her expectantly.

"We're pregnant, darling, isn't it wonderful?"

For the second time in a minute the expression on his handsome face changed. This time to one of shock and joy. His hand slid to her belly. "Our baby...?" His voice of wonder reached the core of her being.

"I'll go to the doctor as soon as we get back to Tylissos. But as much as I want to make love to you right now, I can't."

Suddenly she rolled off the bed and hurried into the bathroom and was sick. He followed her in to help her.

"What can I do for you?"

She rinsed her mouth and face before turning to him with a faint smile. "I think you've already done it, big time." He helped her back to the bed. "But I do have one more favor."

"What is it? I'd do anything for you."

"Promise you won't make too much fuss."

"I promise I'll try to take this in my stride."

"Liar," she teased.

"I only want to take the best care of you and the baby," said Takis. "That's why I took you here."

"And it was a beautiful surprise to be brought here to the castello by my Cretan prince. I love you, Takis".

"And I love you too, Lys," said Takis, "I can't wait to spend the rest of my life with you, my love, my everlasting love."

* * * * *

MILLS & BOON®

Hardback – July 2017

ROMANCE

The Pregnant Kavakos Bride	Sharon Kendrick
The Billionaire's Secret Princess	Caitlin Crews
Sicilian's Baby of Shame	Carol Marinelli
The Secret Kept from the Greek	Susan Stephens
A Ring to Secure His Crown	Kim Lawrence
Wedding Night with Her Enemy	Melanie Milburne
Salazar's One-Night Heir	Jennifer Hayward
Claiming His Convenient Fiancée	Natalie Anderson
The Mysterious Italian Houseguest	Scarlet Wilson
Bound to Her Greek Billionaire	Rebecca Winters
Their Baby Surprise	Katrina Cudmore
The Marriage of Inconvenience	Nina Singh
The Surrogate's Unexpected Miracle	Alison Roberts
Convenient Marriage, Surprise Twins	Amy Ruttan
The Doctor's Secret Son	Janice Lynn
Reforming the Playboy	Karin Baine
Their Double Baby Gift	Louisa Heaton
Saving Baby Amy	Annie Claydon
The Baby Favour	Andrea Laurence
Lone Star Baby Scandal	Lauren Canan

0617 GEN STD HB

MILLS & BOON®

Large Print – July 2017

ROMANCE

Secrets of a Billionaire's Mistress	Sharon Kendrick
Claimed for the De Carrillo Twins	Abby Green
The Innocent's Secret Baby	Carol Marinelli
The Temporary Mrs Marchetti	Melanie Milburne
A Debt Paid in the Marriage Bed	Jennifer Hayward
The Sicilian's Defiant Virgin	Susan Stephens
Pursued by the Desert Prince	Dani Collins
Return of Her Italian Duke	Rebecca Winters
The Millionaire's Royal Rescue	Jennifer Faye
Proposal for the Wedding Planner	Sophie Pembroke
A Bride for the Brooding Boss	Bella Bucannon

HISTORICAL

Surrender to the Marquess	Louise Allen
Heiress on the Run	Laura Martin
Convenient Proposal to the Lady	Julia Justiss
Waltzing with the Earl	Catherine Tinley
At the Warrior's Mercy	Denise Lynn

MEDICAL

Falling for Her Wounded Hero	Marion Lennox
The Surgeon's Baby Surprise	Charlotte Hawkes
Santiago's Convenient Fiancée	Annie O'Neil
Alejandro's Sexy Secret	Amy Ruttan
The Doctor's Diamond Proposal	Annie Claydon
Weekend with the Best Man	Leah Martyn

0617 GEN STD LP

MILLS & BOON®

Hardback – August 2017

ROMANCE

An Heir Made in the Marriage Bed	Anne Mather
The Prince's Stolen Virgin	Maisey Yates
Protecting His Defiant Innocent	Michelle Smart
Pregnant at Acosta's Demand	Maya Blake
The Secret He Must Claim	Chantelle Shaw
Carrying the Spaniard's Child	Jennie Lucas
A Ring for the Greek's Baby	Melanie Milburne
Bought for the Billionaire's Revenge	Clare Connelly
The Runaway Bride and the Billionaire	Kate Hardy
The Boss's Fake Fiancée	Susan Meier
The Millionaire's Redemption	Therese Beharrie
Captivated by the Enigmatic Tycoon	Bella Bucannon
Tempted by the Bridesmaid	Annie O'Neil
Claiming His Pregnant Princess	Annie O'Neil
A Miracle for the Baby Doctor	Meredith Webber
Stolen Kisses with Her Boss	Susan Carlisle
Encounter with a Commanding Officer	Charlotte Hawkes
Rebel Doc on Her Doorstep	Lucy Ryder
The CEO's Nanny Affair	Joss Wood
Tempted by the Wrong Twin	Rachel Bailey